God Bless,
I hope you like it.

Teresa Stutso Jewell
2020

My Bucket's Got a Hole in It

TERESA STUTSO JEWELL

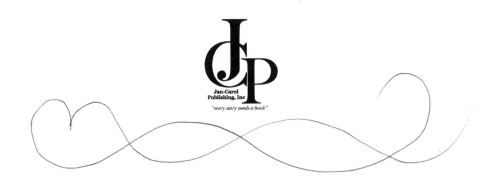

Jan-Carol
Publishing, Inc
"every story needs a book"

Always keep an open heart . . .

My Bucket's Got a Hole in It
Teresa Stutso Jewell
Published April 2018
Little Creek Books
Imprint of Jan-Carol Publishing, Inc
All rights reserved
Copyright © 2018 by Teresa Stutso Jewell
Illustrations by Teresa Stutso Jewell

ISBN: 978-1-945619-58-8
Library of Congress Control Number: 2018942737

You may contact the publisher:
Jan-Carol Publishing, Inc
PO Box 701
Johnson City, TN 37605
publisher@jancarolpublishing.com
jancarolpublishing.com

I want to dedicate this book to all who love the Appalachian Mountains

Letter to the Reader

Firstly, I want to thank you for picking this book. I hope you find a smile here and there, and also a renewed understanding of the Appalachian spirit. We are a very special people who keep our traditions and our love of place. Ida Mae represents mountain memories and our pride of family, our pride of country, and our respect for God and Nature. Don't ever believe that old saying, "You can never go home again..." Yes, you can!

Acknowledgments

I want to thank Radford University's Appalachian Studies Program, Grace Toney Edwards, and my husband, Ebby Jewell, for re-introducing me to the love of our Appalachian heritage.

I will lift up mine eyes until the hills from whence cometh my help.
– Psalm 121, KJV

Table of Contents

Chapter I

The Invitation

Concord College, Athens, West Virginia: 1970

The best way to tell a story is to start at the beginning. But, before I get into the depth of this saga, let me introduce myself. My name is Steven Weaver. This story started when I was just eighteen years old while attending a small college, in a little southern town of Athens, West Virginia. Concord College was a small college located almost at my back door. Truth be known, I wasn't that good at high school, except for the journalism class, and the other schools I applied for didn't accept my application. At that time in my life, I wasn't mature enough to be placed in the middle of some big college with an even larger city around it; I had never been away from home for any considerable length of time. Eventually, I managed to receive my bachelor's degree in Journalism and Communications. It must have been sheer, dumb luck, and a particular personal interview, that rearranged my destiny forever.

Writing had always been my passion. I had high expectations of writing for a newspaper or a magazine, or even working for a big television station as a script editor. I started out my freshman year at Concord College as a photographer-reporter for the school newspaper, and worked my way up to editor by the time I became a junior. Being recognized upon a couple of occasions for my writing abilities made me realize that I had a nose for news, and was lucky enough to be in the right place and the right time. Guess I got a little puffed up with myself, as I had visions of being a freelance writer

1

for the *Bluefield Daily Telegraph* or even the *Charleston Gazette*. I had made decent grades in all my English and Literature classes, and I had a few great professors who encouraged me to go out into the world and try my hand at professional writing. I didn't want to start out like some dumb cub reporter or some assistant to a sports editor; I figured that I had paid my dues. I remember that day that Concord College received a special invitation to be a part of an interview with a one-hundred-year-old woman I had never heard of, or anyone else for that matter.

The local and regional news channels were buzzing about a story of an old woman living up in the thick, dark hills of West Virginia. I recall seeing her face on Channel 6 and hearing her say that she would not allow any professional interviews. I let it go as just some silly, local story that was not worth my valuable time and effort. When I got into my journalism class that next morning, my professor, Dr. Jacob Summers, was excitedly handing out papers that informed us all about that old, white woman who lived up some dark hollow in West Virginia. It seemed that the old woman had now made national and international news press, and all the buzz was over a family's history that dated back to the Colonial days, and how her family lived secretly on top of a mountain. This woman was a hundred years old! There was another twist to the story. It seems a black family from Detroit Michigan and some part of Canada had some connection with this old woman, and they wanted to meet her personally. Dr. Summers said that this was the type of human interest story the public needed at that particular time, because of the tension between the races, and the continuing problems up north and down south. He continued to shout and pace and finally, turned and faced us, and with a pointed finger said, "What this country needs right now is a good human-interest story. We need to take our minds off war and riots! Maybe people want to hear something refreshing for a change, and not see race riots or dead soldiers on some foreign soil during their morning coffee or their suppertime news."

It seems, being hounded to death by the media, the old lady finally told them that she would tell her story one way and on one condition. She said to a television reporter from NBC that she would share her story on Saturday morning of the ninth day of May, at 9:00 a.m., and she would only talk to college students who were interested in the study of the history of Appalachian culture.

Dr. Summers paced quickly all around the classroom and was more animated than I had ever seen him. The sweat had popped out on his lip and forehead, and his shirt was getting wet in his armpit area. His hair was standing up as he kept taking his hand through it, and waving the papers around in the air. He wanted this story. He was wild-eyed as he said, "This story is a true historical account of the colonies, and the determination of the American Spirit that led to the homesteading of the Appalachian Mountains. Don't you understand what I am saying here?"

At that time, no one was interested in anything that had to do with Appalachia; it seemed it was not the "coolest" place to be, and the greater percent of the class couldn't wait to leave the "hillbilly" stigma or the state, for that matter.

Dr. Summers said, as he paced quickly around the table, "*Life* and *Look* magazines want dibs on this article. Do you dumbasses know what that means?"

He took another deep breath. "Guys, I'm telling you all, this could be a chance of a lifetime," Dr. Summers said as he high stepped past me.

"This would bring a lot of attention to Concord College and a considerable amount of attention to whoever got the best interview. All the television stations are interested in this human-interest story," my editor excitedly pleaded with us.

I swear, I thought he was going to have a heart attack or a stroke or something. Summer's face was red; his eyes were wide; his voice was loud and high pitched. I had never seen him like this before. He was all but foaming at the mouth at this point.

The electricity that he was projecting magically flowed from his "charged" body to mine. I knew this was going to be my interview; I saw dollar signs. I'd be famous! None of the students wanted to even try, except me. Not a big surprise, as most of my classmates were from New Jersey or Virginia Beach anyway, how could this interest them? They just wanted to get their schooling over and head to the beach.

After practically attacking Summers and telling him how desperate I was, he knew my ambition. He gladly fudged on my application and stated that I was a history student so that I could get the dibs on this story. I didn't care if it was a little white lie and he didn't either. I just wanted to be read somewhere, anywhere. I had one more semester and man, I was ready to roll. I knew that if this interview could make the front page of major West Virginia newspapers, maybe I could do a little freelance on the side, and perhaps someone might recognize the genius behind the pen (err...typewriter). This opportunity could be my ticket to fame and fortune. I was never as sure of anything in my life as I was then. I had to go. It was my destiny!

My professor gave me a list with questions to ask, gave me a camera with five rolls of film with 24 exposures, a reel to reel recorder, a bag full of size D batteries, a hand-drawn map, and some bug spray. I could not sleep at all that night because of all the visions of the interview going around in my head, as well as questions I needed to ask, and trying to prepare myself to be as professional as I could be.

I woke up early, before my alarm, hours before the sun could peep into my bedroom. I had put gas in the car the day before, bought the stuff I needed, looked at my inventory list, and put all my stuff in the car.

In the square, white, styrofoam cooler, which usually held a six pack of Buds, I packed a few Dr. Peppers, a couple of bologna sandwiches and eight Reese's Cups, and filled the rest of the space with cubes of ice I got from the motel down the street. My aunt worked the front desk, so she let me have ice anytime I wanted it. I placed my survival kit in the backseat of my car along with a paper bag with a few bags of potato chips, three Slim Jims, and some peanuts. After all, I was going up into the mountains, and I didn't know what to expect.

It Begins...

Somewhat excited, I pulled out of my driveway at six-o'clock that morning while the spooky, low laying fog was still on the ground. At the time, I thought that it might be a bad omen, but I put that foolishness down to the scary movie I watched a couple of nights before. Nothing was going to stop me now. I drove with such confidence and focus; I can only compare the feeling to a brave knight going to the Crusades. I knew that I would conquer this story with the greatest of ease. My journey should take approximately three hours from my apartment to Slip Creek; I didn't mind the drive at all, as I considered it a new adventure. I would just put a couple of my favorite tapes in my car and cruise on down the highway, go on up that mountain, get my interview, come home, write it up, turn it in Monday morning in journalism class, and get an easy 'A' for the semester. I had butterflies twittering around in my gut just knowing how easy this interview would be, and of course, the joy of getting away from campus only for a day.

I followed the map that Dr. Summers made for me, and finally found Route 52, then State Route 16 south. There on my right was a little green sign letting me know that I had crossed the Mercer County line and entered McDowell County. Reading the map as I traveled, I saw that just a short way down the road I had to pass a garage on the right and a "Church of Jesus Christ The Anointed," then to turn right after the big bridge that crossed a black, swift-running creek. I turned on a road that snaked its way through some little community that followed a sulphur smelling, willow edged creek. After I crossed a few one-lane bridges, the road turned left up a steep mountainside; on an almost secretly hidden road, there was an old dilapidated sign that read "Slip Creek." I turned left on Slip Creek Road, and then traveled slowly on up the hollow, where I was to find my destiny, at Slip Creek, West Virginia.

The road I turned onto was a dirt and gravel road that went straight up the side of a mountain, into what looked like a green tunnel, as the trees stretched out their limbs above me. There were only a few scattered rays of sunlight pushing their way down through the thick foliage, giving the illusion of a dotted road that splattered the light on the crumbled clay and rocks. I drove up the dusty road that was just barely large enough for my Volkswagen, and prayed that nothing else was traveling down this mountain road to meet me. The ruts were deep and "wash-boarded," and a few times I thought that my car would not make it up the mountain without losing my oil pan or my clutch. I drove slowly and cautiously, which was against my natural habits.

There wasn't the first guard rail or wooden post to prevent a car misjudging the edge and going over a steep ravine. The only thing to stop a vehicle from being lost would be the trees that were side by side all the way down the mountain. The dry, powdered dirt boiled up behind me and lay like a grey, woolen sweater on the green leaves that hovered close to the road. All the foliage that hugged the road had that spooky gray covering. It looked like a clue to a mystery – if someone passed by here, the dust let you know. Even though it was only spring, the forest was thick and dark as I tried to see through it. I couldn't make any speed at all on this dangerous road. About halfway, I found a wide spot ahead and turned off just to let my car rest. I got out, opened my cooler, and got myself a bologna sandwich and a cold drink. I walked around my car and thought about the car wash that was going to get my business as soon as I got down off this mountain, and then as I ate, I listened. It was quiet except for some birds chirping. The fog that was lifting in globby patches seemed to be hanging on some of the trees, near the tops of other ridges that were joining where I was standing. I could see rock cliffs peeking out through the lifting fog and looking like magnificent fortresses. There were hundreds of birds flitting from mountain to mountain, tree to tree, as I invaded their peace.

The air seemed or smelled damp, yet I could tell it was dry by the dust. The whole area carried the same smell as the thick forest that was all around me. If the roadway had not been cut out, it would have looked like no man had ever seen this place or could find it. I imagined that this landscape was the way it looked to the first people who ever walked through here. I could not see a telephone pole or a wire or a cut out except for the road that I was on. From where I stood looking over the landscape, I could not see a thing that had been touched by the hand of man. It was disturbing to me knowing that someone could get lost up here, never be found, or never heard from again. Dr. Summers never mentioned this part of getting the interview. I started thinking, what if I died here by some terrible accident, no one would know what happened. Pulling out my Kodak camera, I loaded the first roll of film and took a few pictures of the lush mountainside, just in case if someone were to find the camera and look at the pictures, they would know where they could find my body.

It was getting warmer, but I didn't know if I was sweating from the heat or the fact that panic was about to take over. Even the temperature of the breeze had a spooky feel. It would change in waves, depending on which way the wind was blowing and if I was in the shadows or sunlight. Even though there was a quietness of the mountains, the quiet was loud.

Man, I thought I was born in the Appalachian Mountains, but I didn't have a clue how thick and dense these mountains were way up here in another atmosphere. I could see from ridge top to ridge top, and through that gray-blue haze, I saw hawks and a couple of buzzards just free-floating with the air stream. This place would have been the perfect location for a movie that had Indians or dinosaurs in it. It still gives me chills when thinking about it, even now. I got back into the car, switched tapes; Credence Clearwater Revival blasted "Proud Mary" and "Born on the Bayou," and it was cranked out. Who would it bother? Being extremely loud and noticed was the objective. All predatory creatures needed to be scared and maybe take an alternative path. I did not want to see any snakes, spiders, lizards, wild cats, wolves, bears, or a T-Rex. Now thinking back, John Denver's music would have been appropriate, but not as loud as it needed to be at that moment. Man, that music sounded great as the journey continued the slow climb on up Slip Creek Mountain. Even now, when any songs of CCR are played on the radio, it reminds me of my travels up and into the heart of the mountains.

The road continued to twist and turn and then clearing, and I finally noticed some daylight that could be seen peeping through the trees. There, as I went further up where the trees were not as dense, they seemed to part like a dark green, lace curtain. There before me was the most significant, real log cabin I had ever seen. I quickly turned off my loud music, because I am sure everyone there heard it fifteen minutes before I arrived. The sight after the dust cleared was breathtaking. The only way to describe my first view was like looking at something sacred. It had a "holy" sense about it, and history dripped from every blade of grass or tree leaf.

I Arrive, Alive!

I was at the top of the mountain, and as far as I could tell, there was not a summit any taller than where I was at that moment. This mountaintop must have been a vast plateau, as it was somewhat flat and seemed to gather all the sunlight along with the sweetest, most refreshing breeze. The cabin was aglow like a bronze castle in the sun's bright, morning light. I parked my car beside the gravel road leading up to the log castle. I just could not believe my eyes as I observed this wondrous sight. I felt like a character in *The Wizard of Oz* or *Alice in Wonderland*. I had never seen anything as beautiful as what I was observing at that very moment. The grass all around it was the brightest green I had ever experienced. Walking on it felt like a very plush carpet, and I could feel the coolness of it through my sneakers.

To say the cabin was unique is an understatement. If you looked real close, you could see where the family had added at least three or four other cabins to it. It was huge. I had never seen a log cabin that had a second story to it. Of course, when I think about it, I had never seen a real, hand-built, log cabin before. I could tell there was apparently an upstairs; with all the windows, it had to have had at least five bedrooms. There was a wraparound porch that covered the front of the cabin and the two sides, which gave a colonial or even southern antebellum look to the cabin. Anyone would have a hard time calling it a cabin. There were other buildings close to the home; a few buildings had to be for storage of some kind and even, I assume, a guest cottage. It was amazing to me to see the beautiful, scientific manner. The mortar between the logs was simply brilliant in some way. The stonework all around the bottom of the house and along the large porch was impressive. From where I stood, one could see at least four chimneys built of that beautiful stone. There wasn't any sign of age, or weathered logs, or ragged rooftops. It looked very professionally made. The architecture of the building just blew my mind. I wondered, to myself, who was the genius, who was the wizard who created this unbelievable place?

There were four cars already parked in the shade by the log house when I pulled up, and I chose to park under a big oak beside the road that would provide shade all day. The area in front of the cabin was flat and well mowed. The lawn stretched all the way to the massive barn that was just to the left of the house, and a few smaller buildings there beside it. Right before the porch, there was a spacious, rounded flower garden planted and surrounded by a river rock-walled edging. Everything was in bloom, and the perfume was almost overwhelming. Being above the frost line does have its advantages. Trees were close to the back side of the house to block the wind, weather, and the harsh evening sun.

There were six girls and three guys drinking from the century-old pump located a couple of yards from the side of the cabin. I walked up to the other students as professional as I could walk, toting my bag full of batteries, cameras, and notebooks, and trying to keep my hair in place. I talked to them a few minutes and introduced myself, and found out their names and schools. They had just arrived about fifteen minutes before I did, and they had not walked up to the cabin porch yet.

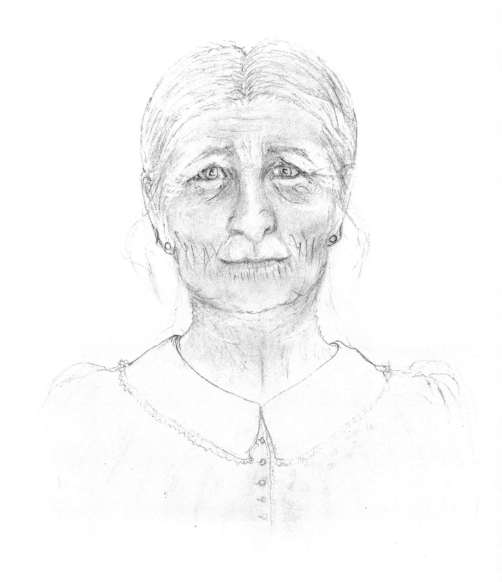

To every thing there is a season,
and a time to every purpose under the heaven:

Ecclesiastes 3:1 King James Version (KJV)

Chapter II

Ida Mae Cook

We walked up the sturdy wooden steps that led to the long, covered porch. I looked around to find a comfortable chair and to find a vantage point, claimed the chair, put down my gear and walked over and saw Ida Mae looking at me through the screened door. The old door was weathered and aged, making it difficult to get a good look at her, and I could tell she was trying to read the name tag that I had just stuck to my shirt.

She opened the squeaky screen door and said to me, "Sugar, are you the young man from Concord College?"

Answering her and trying to sound important, "Yes ma'am, my name is Steven Weaver, and I am here for the interview."

I pointed to my name tag, put my finger on Concord College, and drew my finger across to the title "West Virginia History." I thought I passed inspection and felt stupid and a little guilty for pointing at that sticker. There was a clipboard on the wall next to the door that had all the names of the students that were to be there for the interview. She came with a pencil and checked my name as being present. I passed.

She said in a perky and robust voice, "Welcome to Slip Creek!"

She turned and looked at me and said, "I'm Ida Mae Cook. Some people call me grandmaw Cook, some call me Mrs. Cook, some call me mom-maw, but you young people can just call me Ida Mae if you want to. I answer to them all, don't matter no how."

I turned back and answered her quickly said, "Thank you."

She gave me the sweetest, kindest smile. The girls went up to her so that she could check their names off the page on the clipboard.

She was not alone in the house. I noticed another old lady standing in the kitchen, washing dishes. Ida Mae said, "That old woman in the kitchen is my daughter, Jenny." I looked at her in surprise as she began to laugh out loud.

A voice came through from the kitchen, "Thank you, mother dear."

She also explained in a prideful voice, "I also have a few grandsons and nephews, painting a couple of the back bedrooms upstairs. You probably won't even see the boys today, and there are a couple of granddaughters up there too, changing the beds and dusting, cleaning windows, you know, stuff the family won't let me do anymore."

"You may see a couple of great-grandchildren running around here or a couple of great-nieces and nephews. They're picking cherries this morning before the blue jays get them all. Someone is always here repairing something, mowing, farming, or eating. Yes sir'ree, this here's a busy house," she said with a little cackle.

"Ya'll go on over there and grab you a chair; there's plenty of sitting room."

There was more than enough room, as this was the longest covered porch I had ever been on in my life! I bet there were at least twenty newly painted, white chairs, stools, and rocking chairs, sure enough. All the tables and chairs looked handmade. The furniture was well built, and there were bentwood chairs and tables along with a couple of rockers and benches. While I was looking around on the porch, five more vehicles pulled up. Because of the powdered, flour-like, dust that fell on their cars; one could not tell the color or even read their tags. All the vehicles were the same gray, dusty film of road dirt that made all the cars look equal.

"Ya'll get yourself a good drink from the pump, refresh yourself, and come on up here on the porch, I'm about to get started," she called to the newcomers.

After they drank from the pump, everyone got up on the porch; we had as many on that porch as were in my journalism class. We all got settled, and the coolness of the mountain breeze gently waltzed in and swished lightly on our faces. We were refreshed and comfortable. Ida looked at her audience. There were many names on the sign in sheet that did not attend, but when I did a head count, I came up with twenty-two students. We did fill the porch and the steps just right. Ida Mae came from the screened room, letting the screen door slam behind her. She walked carefully and unassisted to her rocker. We all knew it was her rocker, as it had pretty pillows on it. She looked around, and a smile and warmth came across her face that could have shamed the sun. She addressed us like a seasoned professor at the college.

"Young ladies and gentlemen, my name is Ida Mae Cook. I am one hundred years old, and I have lived here all my life, as did my mama and daddy, and their families, and so forth, starting around the mid-1600's. Where do you people want me to start?"

Once upon a time, long ago...

I quickly jumped in, as I couldn't wait for the others while they looked at one another. I spoke first, "I heard you have journals and records of most of your ancestors, is that true Mrs. Cook?"

She answered, "Yes sir'ee, I have over seven hundred journals. These journals were written by my ancestors. I lent the State of West Virginia one hundred journals, and they put them under glass in the West Virginia State Capital building. I also let the State of Virginia take one hundred of the earlier journals. You all did know that this country was all Virginia at one time, didn't you? They got all hot and bothered over the break up of the nation. It seems they couldn't agree on certain policies, so, they just up and said 'the hell with it all, we'll make a new state and leave you idiots to your own.' Those lovely people from Virginia and West Virginia were kind enough to copy each journal and of course, a copy for themselves."

She went on as she raised her hand to us, "Now mind you, I just lent them to the state history people to copy, and to let the public see them for a while. They do not own them; they just wanted to look at and study the journals. They said that they were very historic and priceless, and they said that it was an important part of our country's history, and of course

West Virginia's and Virginia's History. That made the family so proud. How could I refuse those officials when they put it like that? Knowing this makes the Meade's, the Jewell's, and the Cook's family story go down in history," she said with a hint of pride.

She also included in her statement, "Now when I leave this old world, my family will have all rights to those historical journals and manuscripts. There is a lawyer involved with all this historic treasure, I wanted to make that clear, but I just don't want anybody to have my journals, they belong to my family and their bloodline to treasure, just as I have."

I had to speak up again to show off my superior, inquisitive mind, "How did your ancestors learn to read and write, considering that time in history when practically no one wrote or even read, and how did they get to America in the first place?"

She smiled and sat back and said, "Boy, you are full of questions, and you are getting a little ahead of me, so let me start at the beginning. First of all, they all could read and write. A few of them had left home to get a formal education and then came back and taught the ones left at home. Now mind you, it was not all English that they read and taught. It was some old English, some Latin, and even Celtic that they used in the beginning. In a few of the first couple of journals, it was noted that a few of the family men taught French. They learned to read law and poetry, along with a lot of ballads and religious songs. Later, they all secretly read the Bible that had been printed in German and in French, and they taught each other to scribe or cipher. They were a rare family. They were Irish and Scot, and eventually moved to England in 1601 with the aid of Robert Cecil, who was King James' best friend. It a was common feeling that in a more than a few of the diaries, the Irish did not like the English people. They didn't care for their King either, but when King James moved from Ireland to become King of England, he took his trusted people with him because he didn't trust a lot of the English people. It took a lot of quick talking to make the family move from Ireland. Let me think, if I remember correctly, the Cook and the Meade families worked for the King and were with him long before he married his wife, Anne. There was plenty of gossip about that old boy, but that's another story, and I ain't here to talk about King James."

She said with a smile, "Well, let's see. Nuallán Cook and his sons, along with some of the Sean Meade families, were known by near and far as the best horse and dog breeders in all of Ireland. King James had seen them work with a competitive Duke or Squire, or something like that, and the Duke had won a couple of horse races and hunting competitions. Now, during this time, James was waiting to become King of England. All he had to do was wait 'till Elizabeth died, and he would cleverly just step in.

"While young James The First was still in Ireland, he made friends with the families. It seems he went to a celebration trying to win favor with the local folks; a riot broke out. Thirteen-year-old Ruarc Cook helped saved the King by hiding the King and his men in a cave behind his father's cottage and barn. The King was thankful; he offered the whole clan a way to get out of their poverty. When it came time for the young King to come of age, he never forgot his promise. The Cooks and the Meades, kin and tied together through marriage, were all moved to England for a promised better life."

She continued explaining. "Because of the promised protection of the King, their homes were close to the castle and no one ever bothered them."

Ida May went on with her story, and we fell under her spell as she continued. She told us that on the east, vine-covered side of the castle, there was a secret door which led through a garden that had a walkway covered with greenery leading to the back side of the families' cottages.

The King found great comfort and pleasure slipping from the castle in the evening to visit Nuallán Cook's cottage with all the family, and Sean and Elva Meade's, whom lived side by side, and having a cup of tea with the best scones anywhere. Sean's wife, Elva was sister to Nuallán's wife, Jillian, and Sean and Nuallán were first cousins, so the two families were very close.

"King James The First, loved poetry and theater, and he had a good time at the cottages reading and listening to the two families perform for him. The King would bring armloads of books and papers, as well as tea cakes and little trinkets for them all to enjoy. I still have a couple of the things he gave to the children. They loved to play act and recite way up into the evening. They would laugh and speak of God, witchcraft, and what was right or wrong according to the King. After an extended visit, the King would secretly go back to his castle with scones in his pockets, and no one knew the better."

We watched intently as Ida Mae took a few seconds to think. She would look up to the trees as if she got the stories from an outside assistant, then turn her head back to us, and start telling us those hypnotic stories right where she left off.

"The clans had become close friends as well as an important tool for the King. Both clans were tied to the service of the King for a few years. Two young men, Bram, and Conaire of the Cook family, taught the royal children how to ride properly. It was young Rurac, Dolan, and Fionn, who showed a few of those royals how to breed horses and hunting dogs the right way. It was Gilroy and Irv from the Cooks, and Kenneth, Fergus, and Aedan from the Meade family who helped design the royal stables, barns, and kennels for the Crown of England. They worked closely together, as there wasn't anything they could not design or build. Tara, Shona, Myrna, and Jilleen Cook were governesses, nurses, and teachers to the children of the court, and Fiona, Alma, Derry, Caireann, and Deirdre Meade were just old enough to be housemaids. The King made sure that everyone had a place and something to do within the walls of the King's castle, and even outside of it as well."

We can do better than this...

As Ida Mae talked, we learned that the Cook family along with the Meade family had long heard the King talk about traveling to the 'new world' and had seen the big ships themselves, with great wonder and curiosity. The King asked the family leaders about things they would send on his ships and they would tell him the things people would need for basic survival. The conversation planted the seeds of many ideas in both families, and they dared to imagine what wondrous things were possible later for them. They soon wanted very much to leave England, and try their luck with homesteading and making a new place for the families in the New World. They knew that the King needed them, and they also knew that getting a passage to leave would be a great task. They put their heads together and found a credible plan, and presented it to the King. They used flattery and used the suave term, 'your great foresight as a sovereign,' to plead their case. They were turned down the first time, because the King said that they were needed there, with him. They approached him once again. They reminded him how skilled the clan was and how they could do so many things that the colonists did not know. They swore undying allegiance to the King and all he stood for, and said they would be loyal representatives of his Majesty's wishes. The colonists were unskilled and fundamentally inept in survival skills and in daily works of a fort. They finally finished their pleas by saying, 'Who else can save this colony from perishing, but our clan?'

They also played on the competitive nature of the King, as he wanted to be the first in everything. The Meades and the Cooks told him they could make the fort a perfectly safe and pleasant place, sending with every new ship, records of advancement and growth. King James wanted the people educated and knowledgeable of how to manage to make a vast colony and make this new land an extension of England. The families would bring education to the settlement. King James sent them on his ship, loaded to the brim with everything a growing colony would need. He made them use different names on the ship's registry, in case anyone would recognize the names and know they were spies for the crown. Ida Mae said that the King was pleased with himself that he had made such a deceptive plan.

We all watched and listened so intently, as we were submerged entirely in her stories of the two families and how they plotted to get what they wanted.

She stopped just a moment, took a drink of water, and continued.

"While I am talking about the Cook family and the Meades, let me finish introducing you to those clans. The Cook family consisted of Nuallán and his wife Jillian, Bram, Conaire, Rurac, Dolan, Fionn, Gilroy, Irv, Tara, Shona, Myrna, and Jileen. The Meade family consisted of, Sean and Elva Meade, Fiona, Alma, Derry, Caireann, Deirdre, Colleen, Big John, little Sean, Michael, and Thomas."

Ida Mae stopped again, shifted herself in the chair, and took another drink of water that she set on the table next to her. "My mouth gets a little dry when I talk this much. Do you all want to take a break right now, or should I just go on with my rambling?"

We all said in unison, out loud, "Please go on, Ida Mae!"

Chapter III

The New Beginning

T here were forty of my kin who came to England from their ancestral homes in Ireland and Scotland, and out of those, the King sent only thirty for his service in the new world. The older ones and cousins of the clans were glad to stay in England, and some went back to Ireland and Scotland. There were approximately seventy passengers on that ship, and some of the passengers worked and assisted on the ship as crew." She stopped, shifted her pillows, and began to tell us of the long sea voyage of her family.

She said that even on the long journey across the sea, her family had writing and reading classes. They brought with them some primers and hidden catechism for the children in Latin, German, French, and Greek. They read every waking moment, and the King had made sure they had the best of books, the newest maps, the latest plays, and manuscripts to read. He also sent a lot of paper and scrolls of parchment and tools to bind them so they could report back all the news of the progress in the colony.

It seems at the very beginning, before they had been a week on their long journey, they met a family on the ship whom they found to be good people. She smiled as told the story of meeting the Jewell family. The Jewell Family had sold everything they had to make this journey. The Shamus and Mary Jewell family, who were all educated and loved music, and had raised nine, tall, strapping, black-haired sons with another on the way. Their names are in one of the first journals about the first week at sea. Their names were Blair, Angus, Brian, Faolan, Liam, Daniel, Jonathan, Marcus, Samual,

Osgar, and the one on the way would be named Duncan. It was common knowledge that they would jump up to dance a jig as quick as they would jump into a brawl, and loved to do both with a passion. They were all tall folk and strong as any bear, just like the Meade's. The wives, Mary Jewell, along with Elva and Jillian, became very close as they worshiped together, and doctored their sick young ones together, as well as other people on the ship. Ida Mae reported that she had read in a couple of the journals that the families became fast friends and loyal to each other to the death.

Evidently, the family of farmers and those that were used to hills and countryside were not so fond of the sea. Naturally, being the Atlantic Ocean, there were some terrible gales and rough seas, and a lot of the passengers got very seasick; after the turbulent waves and bad weather passed, the families began to feel better. Ida Mae also enjoyed telling us about a few scuffles with the ship's men and some of the Jewell boys, but she said that they settled their differences quickly.

There was one minor problem with the food and the way it was prepared. To solve the issue, it seems the women took over the galley and helped the cook quite a bit. We all laughed as she told us about how the women and a couple of the boys tied the ship's cook to a post and washed him down, as well as the galley. She chuckled as she told us that the story was added to the daily journal that the cook didn't put up much of a fight with anything done in the galley because he was a little man, and the women were a foot taller than he was and a heck of a lot more powerful. After they wrestled down the cook and cleaned everything from top to bottom, and dared the captain to interfere, Ida Mae said that she knew there was much prayer on the ship deck that day. I would bet, she was probably right! She told us that during that trip with all the kids and women, and other sailors, there had to be other little things that happened. I just cannot imagine after four long, nerve-racking months at sea, the way they all felt when they heard their ship's captain call, "land ho," and they finally landed in a place not too far from what history calls the Chesapeake area.

After listening for a good hour, I am sure we all felt like we had just watched a great movie. We soon gathered our composure and settled back down to our learning and listening. Ida Mae got up and stood for a minute, straightened out her dress, put the pillow just right behind her back, turned and smiled.

The Landing

"I want to start talking about the year 1611. Their ship anchored in a shallow cove on the coast of Virginia." She continued to tell us about what happened next and retold the story with a serious voice. She knew these stories like the back of her hand.

Although they had braved the perils of the ocean, sickness, and boredom, they didn't have a clue what awaited them. Even though there was an English settlement already there, it was written in a few of the earlier journals, that the English people had arrived about eighteen months before and had almost starved to death after one of their leaders left them with only a few other officers. The settlers were left to fend for themselves with a somewhat small group of military men. They didn't know anything about winter gardens and were not very efficient in hunting big game. Ida Mae said if it hadn't been for the Monacan Indians, and a few of the friendly Potomac and Cherokee Indians, they would have all died of starvation or frozen to death!

They were all on the edge of giving up when the ship arrived carrying Ida Mae's family, the Jewells, a naval captain, and his men that were needed to save the whole place. She said she had read that there had been others that were afraid of another winter and tried to run off, and when they came back, they were hanged for treason by the King's military, whom were left to run things. The settlers were afraid of their appointed leaders, and were fearful for their future in this new place.

The weary travelers entered the fortress and saw the sad group of colonists there. As they made their way into the fort, they noted that the fort area was not taken care of, as it appeared to be filthy. They saw dirty water barrels and unkempt grain barrels with traces of rodents and other pests. There was not even an infirmary, a doctor, or anyone who could assist. As Ida Mae had read the journals, she said the people there were in dire straits, and it was not what her family thought it would be.

When the clan walked around in the fort, they told the colonist's leaders that the fort needed to be expanded, but they met with opposition to the idea. The colonists feared that it would weaken their defense during that time of building. Those people had gone through a lot and were scared out of their minds, I guess. The people at the fort had trouble from the very beginning with the leader of a band of warring Indians. They'd also had to fight off a bunch of renegade, eastern shore Indians upon occasions.

Most of the people living there did not have a trade, or were not trained in survival and living off the land. Some knew how to fish, few knew how to build, less knew how to work with metal, and less than that knew how to farm. I tell you, they must have been a sad lot. The main tasks now for the clans were to act like regular pilgrims, and to help and teach all the rest there. They had to make the others believe that they were in a better place than England, Scotland, or Ireland. The people knew that this would be home for the rest of their lives. All the while, Ida Mae's family had to pretend that they were not spies for the King, sort of like double agents. They had to gain everybody's trust to do what they had to do.

The Cooks, the Jewells, and the Meades, saw plenty of unused land to expand outside the walls of the fort, and they liked what they saw. Initially, there were plans and allotted partials for the new families to live and farm outside of the fort, but not one of them would dare live outside of the protection of the fort boundaries.

Thankfully, the colony had already made friends with some of the friendly Indians from the Monacan tribe and some of the Cherokee people. But they had some bad experiences with other wandering and hunting parties that were not so kind or helpful. Thank God, all the Indians were not like that, and some were very friendly. The Cooks, Meades, and the Jewells, as well as the captain of the military group that came, took charge immediately and got down to business, thus basically saved those people and secured their future.

The families found when they got there, there wasn't any room for them to sleep indoors, so they had tents to stay in for a while. The family, all knowing how to do different things, immediately gathered some of the men from the fort, and went out to hunt and trap for game. Some people were charged to start building holding pens and corrals for the new livestock brought in, while others were shown how to construct feed sheds, they also cleared some fields and burned all the trash. Within a few days, they were ready for some of the men to hook up oxen to the plows, and started turning the soil outside of the fort to plant crops. The families, being used to a kinder ground, found the earth in the new world just a little too sandy and what wasn't sand was hard clay. It was hard to plow, and they had to work just a little bit harder to make the crops grow. Every person there that wasn't doing another job had a shovel and a pick to dig out long ditches, so the fresh running stream would come closer to the fort, and they could have fresh water close by and not so close to the outhouses. Privies or toilets were always placed below the fresh water source. They hurriedly constructed a blacksmith shop of stones outside of the fort so it wouldn't burn down already made structures. While some were out gathering river rock and large stones for the blacksmith building, others were bringing in fresh meat every day and brought in roots and berries for food and medicine, more than enough for everyone.

Ida Mae told us that she had read in one of the journals, written by one of the Cook girls, that within a month things were looking like a new place. There was a new hope, and a future where there had been none.

"Every one of my clansmen had a job, and they spread out and taught everyone they could to do specific tasks. The settlers were taught to read, how to write, how to draw maps, how to farm with the seasons, how to make nets, how to fresh water and salt water fish, how to make metal tools, how to heal specific ailments, and what foods to eat and what not to eat. Most of the seeds that came with them were planted. The sections all around the outside of the fort and the new set boundaries already had new fencing. The clans had gained the trust of every living soul there," Ida Mae told us.

The clansmen agreed that things would not have gone so well if it had not been for the friendship and generosity of the friendly Indians they had encountered upon the first week of their arrival. The Monacans made their encampment just a little way from the fort for their protection and for the aid and assistance to their new friends, the fearless clansmen. One Cherokee encampment was about a mile from the fort, and some came and went as they pleased. The Cooks, Meades, and the Jewells within a month, had made close friends with the Monacans. They traded a lot together and learned how to communicate. The Indians had already taught them to hunt and fish in their fashion. The clansmen found the abundance of fish and game and learned how to prepare and dry meat and fish just like the Indians did. It didn't take Ida Mae's people very long before they knew about everything there was to know about the whole area. It seemed there was an unusual blending of cultures that went on that first year.

Although there were many differences in the culture of the strict English and the rough and the unorthodox Irish and Scots; each had their way of doing things as they were taught in their homeland and the natives had their way of doing things on this, their homeland. They all had a common goal, and that was to survive the best way they could. There were many things they taught each other, and they depended upon each other for a new life. They learned each other's languages, medicines, and had great patience with their superstitions, religions, and cultures. It was a good mix and a great learning experience. Ida Mae said that the English women had a hard time learning to do hard work that they had never done, and the Indian women taught them. Everyone had to work hard together for their survival and a future for their children.

****Chapter IV****

The Seasons of Change

S he continued in a seemingly softer voice, and she talked just a little slower. "Winter came with some problems, such as sickness and just keeping things warm. Thank God it was not a bitter winter, and the game did not leave. They all had worked hard together to prepare for the winter. The corn harvest was bountiful, as well as the hay, cabbages, potatoes, and other root vegetables, even apples, nuts, and grains. The sea brought forth great bounty, as did the forests. All seemed to be doing well, yet there was still fear of Indians as tribes of them moved in and out of the area. There were a few skirmishes and threats, which made their fears even stronger. Hardly any of the older people that had been there before trusted the friendly Indians, even though it was through their generosity that they lived as long as they did."

Ida Mae took another sip of water and continued to tell her tale of her ancestors as she rocked in her chair.

It seems as time went on, the fort leaders, including the Meades, Cooks, and the Jewells, wanting to expand and trying to keep down the fears, declared land outside of the fort a safety zone where the colonists could build houses outside the fort if they wished. Not one of those people expressed interest in leaving the safety of those wooden walls. They knew the Monacans and some of the Cherokee had encampments close by, and many of English didn't trust them. So, it was the clansmen who said that, since they did almost all the hunting and had farming skills, they would take it upon themselves to build outside in the safety zone, so they would be closer to the forests and the game. The colonists thought that was a grand idea, and they all agreed that it should be the new people to help settle out there and make it a safer place for all of them. A few of the men from the fort became extra hands early in the morning, but before the sun started to set in the west, they were gone and locked tight in the fortress with their wives and families. It did not take very long for the clansmen to build their log houses and their farms. They moved their tents outside of the fort and stayed there. During the days, they made great fires and cooked for everyone that helped, including the Indians. The Monacans also sought safety with the clan, as they often fought with nomadic wandering natives, and they knew the clansmen were warriors and fearless. The safety zone stretched out about a mile from the fort. The clansmen built on the very edge of the safety zone and one cabin was even off the boundary. No one said a thing about being outside of the fort, or questioned why, or came to visit. The people inside the fort made it very clear that they would not assist them after dark. But Ida Mae's people did help them expand the walls of the fort to double the size, and made room for a few more houses and a building for a school. As the story goes, everything was going very well for all concerned.

Spring was wet the next year, but it brought great bounty with the traps set out farther, and the clansmen and some of the Indians provided elk, deer, raccoon, geese, grouse, squirrels, bear, possums, and skins from wolves, otters, beaver, muskrats, fox, lynx, and mountain lions. The skins gave them excellent trading power with wandering natives. The people in the fort were well satisfied with the way things were going.

The clan families did what they promised to do. They helped with the building of new homes and underground storage places, they taught the blacksmiths to do other jobs, and taught the first organized school there. A couple of ships would arrive about every six months. They brought supplies and oxen, other cattle, and horses, as well as some goats and pigs. The preparations for the voyage back to England took a while as they had to get fresh water, gifts, gathered progress reports, and loading correspondence back to their kinfolk in England, The Meades always received letters from England, secretly from the King, and they in return sent back their reports. News of

England was interesting and they learned of the happenings with the military, of news of piracy on the open seas, and delivery of the new charters written by the King, and seed allotments. There was always a man or two sent from the King to check on everything and everybody. They would stay inside the fort. They had been invited many times to visit with the clan, but quickly refused. They were like scared little rabbits. They couldn't wait to sail back home. As soon as the ships were loaded and restocked with fresh water, those Englishmen would be the first ones ready to go. Some of the King's men would give up and go back home. None ever repeated the trip. This new land wasn't for the faint of heart, for sure!

"The new families taught the others how to plow and plant the right way on this new land, and the Indians taught them how to hunt and stay alive in the winter months. King James I, had received timely reports from the family and the captain, and all seemed to be going very well and the King was very impressed. But, as it is human nature, the more you have, the more you want," Ida Mae said.

I watched her face as she looked intensely into our eyes as she told the story. Her eyes were bright, and she used her hands as she talked. I started taking a few pictures of her as she spoke, which never bothered her at all, nor did it stop a word. She took a good breath and began talking again.

"As could be expected, the King was going to change some of the charters and decrees, and taxes would be more significant. He was going to control how much land a person could own, and he would decide what was grown on it. The King had changed his mind on how things were to be in the new little colony. He had soon become greedy with his little venture, after seeing how great and abundant the land had been described. He insisted that there was gold there. Of course, there wasn't any gold in that wilderness; the only thing that place offered was scrub bushes, pines, sticker bushes, snakes, and bugs. The King also thought that the two families had whiskey stills, as they had always had a keen taste for liquor, and he figured they made their own. The rum the King had sent was of poor quality, made with bad water. He read about the fresh, best-tasting water we had here in this new world. The King wanted half of their product and taxes on the rest. Talk about upsetting a few folks. Rurac let the captain take one of his older whiskey stills. He was assured that there was not another one. The captain would have never found the others.

"The compound outside the fort was growing as more people were moving in every six months, between seasons. The coastline of Virginia and North Carolina proved to be very dangerous, as England lost many lives, provisions, and ships on her rocky coast, as the weather was more changeable and treacherous on this side of the world. The King thought he could make up his loss by raising the taxes and cost of other staples."

We can do this for ourselves, only better!

"The family leaders had long decided they could not swear allegiance to anyone who would purposely hurt his colonists. After some talk about their original plans, they realized that they could not spend another winter in that area with ships coming in with more military and settlers in the fall. The winter was too dangerous to travel on the ocean, so it left them alone without help for the hardest months of the year. Knowing what lay ahead for the colonists, the clans Cook, Meade, and Jewell knew it was time to make a move. They would do what they wanted to do in the first place, just a little sooner than they had planned. They met secretly while looking at maps and giving general observations. It was time to find their own piece of land and live as they knew how. They had carefully made friends with some of the friendlier Monacan and Cherokee Indians there at the fort. In a friendly chat, the Indians told them of land down past the big river, and past the forbidden valley. They said that there was another place that held a mighty river the Indians of those parts called the 'River of Death,' and it ran like a snake to the northwest. The Cherokee had traveled that direction the most, and they said the game was thick as the pine forests, and the mountains would provide everything they needed. The Indians told them if they did not want to be found, the mountains would hide them forever. The Indians had not been treated with respect, and the clansmen were the only ones that treated them kindly and like brothers." She reset herself on the cushion and crossed her legs and rocked back a few times and continued.

"The clan families were prepared, and plans were made. Every evening they sat around the Meades' big table by candlelight and made plans and wrote out timetables. They all knew what they must do, and when to make a 'run for the hills.' They knew the seasons, the wet months, the dry months; they studied the rivers and waterways, the patterns of the flying birds, and the direction the game came and went, and made sure their trust was solid with everyone."

As the story went on, all the preparations for the escape were made quickly. The women were told not to get pregnant during this time, as it would be a hard trek on an infant and worse on a pregnant woman, as that would slow them down. Ida Mae said they did that with help of the Indian women, who had knowledge of such practices and helped with certain herbs. She didn't elaborate on that, but we all just assumed Indians knew the secret. Not another soul knew the plans but the three families, and a chosen group of Monacan Indians that wanted freedom also.

Everyone living in the fort fully trusted them, after all, they were the providers. They planned and plotted like spiders spinning their webs. Every effort or motion was made to benefit the trip. The webs they spun were small at first, but they eventually started to spread out. Because they were the best hunters of the whole compound, they were trusted with bringing in most of the meat for the fort. This advantage let them have the freedom to go and come without question. They went hunting a little farther than they did the week before. They told some of the people that the clan needed to follow the deer and elk as they moved westward, so it was necessary for two and three-day hunting trips, and then up to a week. They would take tools and other things, wrapped in oilcloth so they would not rust or rot, and hid them on their trails way down the line. The people of the fort were so glad when they were stocked up with wine, brandy, hay, corn, wheat, their gardens full, venison, turkey, elk, and dried fish; no one noticed the clans' coming and going.

It was important for the colonists to learn how to preserve food; they learned how to dry meat and fish, as the Indians did. Thus guaranteeing their future, and everyone's confidence of survival during the harsh winters. The colonist and the soldiers were pleased knowing that they would not starve during the late winter time. Ida Mae's ancestors were more than well stocked and ready too. They had packed all kinds of different meats in salt, smoked, dried, and put away. Their Indian friends did the same and taught them many ways of preservation and light travel. They hid their stash of dried food, seeds for planting, and grains all over the place, so when they left, they had plenty of food for the long trip to the mountain range they had heard of from the Indians. They chose the finest young oxen, heifers, bullocks, little pigs, goats, chickens, and horses, all good blood and breeders. They knew that the young would make the trip and struggle a lot less than aged livestock. Of course, they had their good dogs for hunting and their best-breeding horses.

Their Indian companions taught them very well. Something I thought they did that was brilliant, they took a couple of large carts literally loaded, and left them way down the hunting path a week or so before they went for good. They had told the fort that the reason they did not come back with the carts was because the men met up with a wild Indian war party whom burned both carts and everything in them, and they barely escaped with their lives. This made all the other people, including the guards, more afraid than ever of the unknown land beyond the gates. The clan families had planned everything down to the last detail. Every time they went hunting, they would leave a bundle of spun wool, whiskey still parts, tools of all kinds, and other essential gear wrapped up in a hiding place way up in the trees along the way. They knew that once they started with the trek, there would be no turning back. The Indians packed up heavily and left a week or so before the families did, going miles beyond the boundaries. The Indian group took their families, all their necessities, as well as a lot of the clan's things like cages of chickens, geese, and some oxen.

Very early one spring morning, they made their escape. Three hours before the cock crowed, the traveling band of refugees was ten miles away from the boundary line. No one noticed. Because their cabins were on the boundary, and they were always out hunting, it took two or three days, or maybe a week or two, no one knew for sure, for the guards to realize that they were gone. The large carts that traveled behind the animals drug tree branches behind them to mark out any trails, and they tried to stay in the high grassy plains as much as they could. Every animal they took with them, except the sheep and goats, of course, had a bundle to carry on its back. A couple of days after the departure, they experienced a significant storm. It blew in from the direction of the settlement. It rained very hard and washed all their tracks away, and they were never found by the guards, and the Indians that stayed behind never told, I assume. She said that the Indians who traveled with them guided the families past the long river and further on.

One part of this story that stuck with me, Ida Mae told us that one of the men in the group, while traveling on foot, pointed to the horizon and he thought another terrible storm was brewing. The man feared they were storm clouds as the air was getting cooler. What he saw was a purple, misty mountain range, and the Indians told them all that they were not clouds at all, but mighty mountains that were waiting for them to come and live in peace. I can only imagine what those people thought when they saw for the first time that beautiful mountain range. She also said that one of the men had written that the mountains still had some snow on the tops of them, as it was very early spring.

Our host broke our spell by continuing the story, "... in one of the journals a writer wrote, I believe his name was Ethan, that 'they knew how Moses felt when he got his first glimpse of the 'promised land.' They never looked back."

Moving onward and upward...

She told us about one of the young men, Ethan, who wrote that during the whole trip, some walking and some riding, the lessons never stopped. The lessons they learned while traveling were not always from a book, but taught by very experienced teachers. The Indians took on the task to show every soul there about the new world they were entering. They learned about the trees, herbs, cures, insects, birds, reptiles, fish, signs, and all about the land from the Indians. Amazingly, in one of the journals, it was written that the most unusual thing noticed was the dirt. It was different soil. It was rich and dark, and clumped together nicely. The ground had a sweet smell, not like that soil that was too close to the ocean, which had a salty, dirty smell. They all agreed that it smelled like fresh plowed Irish soil. As they walked or rode through the rough country, our host told us that the Bible stories were taught by the elders, and they openly sang hymns and prayed. The Indian children and their parents enjoyed the spoken lessons. She also said, "All the travelers got a good dose of religion!"

She looked around and asked, "Are you young'uns ready?"

We all nodded like little puppets and looked up into her misty blue eyes and watched her mouth. She showed no signs of tiring as she spoke and continued to pull me into her whirlwind.

"I have to tell you one of the most remarkable stunts pulled by these Scots-Irish people was when they left quietly that early morn, they left their houses as if they still lived there. They left the older livestock in the fields and pens with feed, chickens in the yard, and left the furniture and even some old clothing on the line. They also stocked the fireplace with slow-burning wood. There was an Indian's lance stuck in the front door, as to let someone believe they may have all been killed or taken as slaves. It is hard to tell how long a time passed before someone dared to go that far to look for them, or what tales were told about their disappearance. The clansmen knew that they had to be very careful. Even the journals that they wrote in were not touched until they made camp at the base of the first mountain range. They used their heads, all right. They had to do or die."

Guess that was one of the fiercest attributes the family passed down from child to child. She told us about how mountain people are hard to get to know, and it's almost impossible to get them to talk about their lives. They think it is better not to say too much and let everyone know your business. The best policy during those times was to listen and keep your mouth shut. They all learned this from their Indian traveling companions. Ida Mae said that in the past, they were all taught city people and flat landers were so different, that they were all rich and they thought mountain folks were uneducated barbarians and were trash.

She said, "We just judged those people as helpless fools, and prayed they'd just stay home and not venture up to our mountains."

Ida Mae looked around, afraid that we might have seen her serious side and her frown, which quickly turned into the sweetest of smiles. She looked at us again, and after a moment of thought she said, "I have changed my inherited way of thinking now, and I feel we should know each other's worlds and put them together somehow for the betterment of the whole world. People should know how to live off the land, just in case something terrible happened to the cities, which really could happen at any time. When this interview is over, you children promise me you won't look at me in a dim light. Please report that I knew things, and I wasn't ignorant, and I have feelings just like anybody else. Promise you will tell them how wonderful living up here is, and how I would not, or could not have lived anywhere else. Okay?"

We paused and looked at her. I just wanted to kiss her hand. We all talked at once and assured her of our promises.

"We promise you will be proud of what we write, Miss Ida Mae," said the little redhead sitting beside me, and we all agreed in unison. She smiled as she continued her steady rock in her chair.

I had started thinking a little differently than I had anticipated, and it was just the beginning of the interview. Man, what a history lesson this lady had just presented. We all looked around at each other thinking the same thing. The group of students sitting there on that long porch were mainly speechless and entranced by her incredible story. I thought to myself how beautiful it would be to go through those books and read each one of those treasured historic journals; then I realized that the real treasure of the whole story was sitting right across from me. I had looked into the eyes of living history.

Chapter V

The Indians of the Mountains

H oney, you and that little girl beside you, if you will, go into the living room there and just beside the couch on the other side, you will find a wooden crate full of old books. Would you mind bringing them here to me?" Ida Mae asked kindly, as she pointed toward the screen door.

Upon her request, we went inside, got the box, which took both of us and we could have used another to lift it, carried it outside and put it beside her rocking chair. She thanked us, and we went directly to our seats like obedient servants. Then the questions exploded.

That little girl beside me spoke up and said, "What about the native Indians that lived in the mountains where your family first settled?" She asked again, without taking a breath, "Did they have any battles or skirmishes between the red man and the white man?"

"Oh, my goodness," Ida Mae said. "Now, they had a time in the beginning, let me see here" she mumbled as she leaned over to pick up a leather bound book with loose, brown paper.

These were just a fraction of the questions bulleted to Ida Mae. She had read all the books, or had them read to her, since she was three. She could recite almost word for word in every book. She opened the book she had chosen from the pile and brushed her delicate fingers over the page with such respect. She looked at them all and leaned back, rocked forward, and began again.

I can't remember when I first heard the phrase, "Run for the hills!" I know where it came now, and I understand why. Besides the escape from the King's rule to the mountains, and now with the fighting with the Indians, I can only imagine the stress and fear they must have felt all the time.

The Indians were seen from a distance at first, as they just watched them. They were curious about the white man, and they didn't know what the white strangers would do. It seems that the Cook family, along with the Meade's, and the Jewell's made quite a spectacle with their oxen, cows, horses, wooden cages full of chickens, and a passel of noisy children. At the first camp at the base of a vast mountain range, they met with a hunting party of Indians. The Indians ran close to the camp and shouted. The men stood their ground and didn't move, but evidently, the Indians thought it better to make a show and leave. This action, being the first show of aggression, scared the families to death. The clansmen knew not to show any fear to the hunters, after all, it was the first time they had been face to face with an angry, red savage. I am sure it was the first time the red man in that area, had ever laid eyes on a group of pasty white men with flaming red hair, along with those big hairy Jewell men with their thick black hair and wooly beards.

We all laughed at the vision she had presented us with, and the way the Indians looked at the first white men. I had never thought of it that way.

She looked over the pages and then she quickly sat up and said, "Here it says in this older book," as she turned to a page and traced her finger down to the middle of it. "They made a temporary makeshift fortress against a rock cliff, which had a very ample cave. They had few little skirmishes of back and forth hollerin' and throwing rocks, but they were higher up than the Indians were, and the Indians didn't have a chance of hitting any of them. So, they just gave up and left. It was an advantageous spot to survey the surrounding landscape, so every able-bodied man did not fret or worry about danger when they left the others to find the homestead place. The older adults, along with about six Monocan men, women, and older children were all armed, guarded by their hounds, and they had a lookout system, and slept in shifts, and went about their daily chores like making tools and harnesses and gathering. They stayed busy every waking moment. The Indians knew every move they made and seemed to be interested in the newcomers, but very wary of the whole group. Finally, the men folk found just the perfect place, and they started taking tools and other heavy things with them as they traveled back, and forth which took a week to make one round trip. And then, the day came for the families to pack up the kids and animals and move up to the mountains. Some walked, and some rode, because the animals and the wagons were full to the hilt with the family's gear, and everyone had to carry something. Even the children carried sacks of feathers for pillows and bedding on their backs. They didn't have to worry about water, because they followed a creek for five days, and the rest of the time the smaller creeks and streams took care of their thirst. While the men were traveling back and forth, they hunted and found plenty of game. They also had plenty of dried fruit and apples with them, plus all the fresh roots and berries they could find. They ate like kings. The Indians spoke the truth, the mountains gave them everything then and even now."

Our wonderful teacher turned a couple of pages and seemed to scan it quickly. She found something that made her eyes twinkle, and she started again, spinning her tales of the wandering pilgrims.

"The men had encountered yet another group of friendly Monacan Indians, who themselves had to run away from their land in the east. They knew the Indians travelin' with them and were glad to see them, and they too helped the traveling band of weary refugees to get to the homestead area. The Monacan Indians, numbered about thirty at that time, traveled the whole trip with them and continued to stay with them up here on this mountain and in the valley. While the men were going back and forth, they would cut an ample path and fill in some of the holes that would have stopped a wagon with smaller rocks and clay. They knew that the wagons and carts could only go so far. The rest of the way was entirely by foot or by hoof. They would work out the problem of clearing the road, and the dismantle the big wagons later. They used long poles and tied and bound the rope and vines around needed things and drug them behind them in this fashion.

"The cutting and clearing of the logs took almost all summer. The Monocan Indians would come and go like the wind, as it was their nature. If it had not been for friendly Indians, the families would have had it a lot harder and a lot slower."

Don't mess with the wrong people...

Ida Mae picked up another book, opened it carefully, and then held it to her breast. She spoke again just where she left off. We listened and wrote in a fever. She said that she had read that one time, the Monacan Indians came under attack by a hunting party of other Indians, she said the writer wrote that they were Mingo, and they kidnapped one of the children of the Monacan chief.

"Our families got together with our friends, the Monacan Indians, and they went out and fought the Mingo Indians and killed every one of the kidnappers, burned their village, and retrieved the child unhurt. The chief of the Monacan Indians swore to be friends with our families forever. They shared many a supper with one another throughout the years, and could depend on each other no matter what. One of the elders of the tribe, the family called him "Doctor," could cure just about anything on the mountain, be it man or beast. He knew every herb and root in the forest. He was more than willing to teach us everything he knew, and our families took advantage of the offering. The language barrier was soon dissolved quickly, with the children first, and the children taught the parents. "Doctor" helped stop fevers and cured snake bites, and healed many a sore foot on the beasts, as well as the painful muscles of our hard-working men." The writer in the book she was holding even said that he could stop bleeding. The families were never afflicted with plague or smallpox, and "Doctor" could heal with his touch.

The stories rolled from her lips, and she knew each one by heart. I know most of them now. As long as I live, I will never forget these stories as if they were my own. She told the astonishing tale of how they kept their mountain and its inhabitants safe.

"As time passed, other Indian tribes that traveled through looking for game, found the new settlement nestled on the top of a mountain. Some wanted to fight for the land and did not want the white intruders there. Things didn't turn out the way those warriors had planned. Their heads were put on spikes at the base of the hollow, just like they did with the animal's heads. It sounds brutal I know, but it scared any intruders who wanted to venture up the steep, dangerous grounds looking for trouble. Those skulls served as an unmistakable warning. Some Indians just didn't scare that much, and they ended up on the spikes with the others. There were some friendly Indians, some curious, some extremely cautious, and some just plain mean Indians, just like white people. The families had to keep a secretive profile and blend into the forests so they would not be bothered by hunting parties. The clansmen became one with the forest like their red brothers. The family learned to walk in the woods without making a sound, as not to frighten the smallest bird. The hunters only killed what the clan needed."

Ida Mae said that there was an understood, unspoken rule that no one would ever kill for sport, but would in a heartbeat for protection of the family. The ability to find game was never a problem. There were buffaloes, large elk, deer, bear, badgers, beaver, smaller critters, and everywhere there was a mud puddle, it would be full of fish. Eventually, many animals that had broken away from settlers who had tried to come or the ones who just abandoned their quest, the boys would find while huntin' and bring them all back home with them. It seemed all abandoned or orphaned animals found their way to the farm. They had mules, and a couple of well-bred horses wandered in, and some wild cows and oxen were quickly caught and domesticated again. Even a dozen or so pigs were reintroduced to farm life. Ida Mae said that for some reason, all animals loved that mountain.

The family had to keep their place untouchable. Those big boys did some bad things to scare the Indians. Like she said before, the family hung the skeletons and heads of the game or anything that had died naturally or unnaturally, all around the bottom of the mountain, and some close to the river. I heard somewhere, probably from my World History class, that they got that from the Irish and Scot warriors that practiced the same scare tactics. Even some pirates did that along the coasts of secluded islands.

Word got out that the inhabitants of the hollows were "devils or bad spirits," and the other Indians just left them alone. One of the stories that the Indians passed around was that the strangers that lived up there were devils because they had red hair. One time during a "showdown," the Indians came up a little too close for the men's comfort. Ida Mae said that one big man on the Meade side, Jonathan, had a long, red, curly beard. He wet his beard and then oiled up a few twists of hair, then lit the twists of hair with a piece of burning firewood and quickly put it out, which left the beard unhurt, but with smoke coming from it. He came out swinging a large saber and screaming at the top of his lungs. The Indians ran away. I'll bet those Indians thought he was breathing fire. It scared the living daylights out of those not-so-brave braves that day. The warriors believed that fire leaped from the wild devil's heads and out of their mouths like the fire gods. They turned around so fast it looked like they were running backward. Generations around the campfires and fireplaces of their cabins told this entertaining story. Fear and superstition were the smartest weapons the family ever used.

After a while, the Indians just left. Little did the family know that other pioneers were running them off their land and pushing them farther west. I guess that nobody wanted to be so high up the mountain where they could not farm or find food. They had no idea that on the top of that mountain was the most excellent grazing land this side of the Mississippi, and it flattened out in many places and had bountiful valleys and full streams and ponds.

"It was around twenty years after settling that some of the clansmen ran into other whites hunting in the general area. The other settlers had heard of the Cook, Meade, and Jewell families that had mysteriously disappeared. Some wanted to settle close by, but the families just would not allow it. So, unfortunately, those who wanted to go back and tell the soldiers that they knew where the infidels were, ended up on spikes with the other decayed messages. The family knew they had to survive and take care of business, no matter what the color, or the price."

She stopped just a minute to let us check our tapes, and she smiled as we fiddled with our tape machines and tablets. A couple of the girls had to change ink cartridges in their pens. I used an old, cheap, ballpoint ink pen that worked very well. I had a spare in my pocket, just in case. I took some more pictures of her and a few of the students sitting on her long porch. We all had to stand and stretch, and some of us went to our first outside toilet. It was a two-seater and was amazing to us. We all had our laugh and got back to our seats. She was ready to start again, and so was I. She uncrossed her legs and adjusted her dress, and spoke.

"A few years after that, there were twelve good sized cabins and common storage houses and barns spread around the mountain. They all had around about fifty acres around each household, and they worked together and shared in the abundance or famine. They worked together to build fences around it all to keep farm critters in or keep other stuff out."

The best friends, neighbors, and family...

"The friendly Indians that lived close by stayed for years, they were always welcome on the mountain, until they left or died out. They lived there all their lives, and some ventured out into the new world, some stayed to be buried there. Even when Ida Mae was a child, there was a family that still lived on the back side of her mountain, that she knew were Indians, and it was just understood that they were like family and we would help them, or they would help us, always. Her ancestors tried to keep peace with the area Indians, and especially because two of our womenfolk married Indian men.

When Ida Mae mentioned the marriage, there was a moment of hush, and then the 'question bullets' were fired again by all different people.

"Who were the ones that married the Indians?"

"How did that go over with the rest of the clan?"

"Do you have Indian blood in your veins, Ida Mae?"

Ida Mae laughed out loud, slapped her knee, and wiped a tear from her eye from the hard laughter.

She finally cleared her throat and collected herself. She took a breath and looked around and said, "Darlin's, if your families came from anywhere around within three hundred miles of here, the probabilities of having Indian blood is pretty good."

Everybody agreed, chuckled a little, and took time to make sure that they had fresh batteries, and turned the pages in their notebooks.

She stood up and stretched her back and spoke. "Let's drink some iced tea and let me wet my whistle, so I can continue without chocking to death. I ain't talked so much since my cousin from War Mountain came and stayed a week with me."

Ida Mae went into the kitchen and called for a couple of girls to help her carry the pitcher and the glasses, and she told them to set it all down on the little white table that set in the middle of her long porch. Everybody settled down with a tall glass of the best iced tea that I believe, I have ever tasted. She said she didn't have any lemons because the little store down at the foot of the mountain rarely gets them. I could taste lemon in the tea, but there weren't any lemons anywhere. I asked her how she got the lemon taste without lemons, and she said,

"Honey, up here, what you can't find at the store, the mountain will give you. I have a plant that grows wild up here that tastes better than real lemons, and you just brew it with the tea".

Again, we all just looked at each other in total amazement. Even now, in this age of modern machines, ideas, and soft living, God still provides for Ida Mae and her family. But, sitting there on her porch, the present day was years away, and like a time machine, I was experiencing Ida Mae's years in the past and I loved it, we all did. On her porch, the world even smelled different. The scent of honeysuckle and her rambling roses that were on the side of the porch came when the light wind shifted. The fragrance of her freshly hung laundry kept the whole area smelling just as sweet as the flowers. The long supported clothesline was on the other side of the house. The towels and sheets made a slight slapping noise when the ends of the them flapped with a change of the breeze. There wasn't a sound of cars or trucks, no smell of exhaust fumes, no close neighbors or loud voices, just the sound of a nearby bird calling to, I assume, another of his species. I heard a few buzzing bumble bees circling the roses and the honeysuckle. There were butterflies and hummingbirds everywhere. *This looks like a perfect place for a Disney Movie.*

"I noticed," Ida Mae broke the silence, "you listened to that red bird over there in my maple tree."

I turned and looked at her and said, "Yes! I did hear that. What kind of bird is it?" I said like a little child.

She answered quickly, "Honey, that's a cardinal. The call that he is making is the call he uses when he is 'wetting up rain.'"

I was a little confused, and I guess she could see it in my face because she said, "That is a special call he makes when it is going to rain pretty soon. Some old folks said that he could call up the rain and the rain would answer. Cardinals are such blabbermouths; he is telling every critter to prepare for rain."

I listened again, and his call was soon joined by another cardinal as if they were actually communicating.

Ida Mae looked over her shoulder and pointed her finger, saying, "Ha! You see, he's told another, and they both are going to make sure the message gets out! The cardinal has three or more different calls, like when he wants to know if any other cardinal is around in these parts, or he just wants to call to his sweetheart," she said as she giggled again, and then we all laughed and were delighted for the extra information.

"Now, young'uns, let's get back to the Indians and the white women." She said as she wanted to continue without being sidetracked too much. Ida Mae reached for her family Bible and said that it had registered the first marriage outside of the families, was to an Indian man and it happened in the year of our Lord, 1720, and the second marriage happened two years later.

"The girls, both sisters, were kidnapped by a warring band of Iroquois. The girls had traveled with the Iroquois for about two months when another tribe attacked them. The family thought them to be Logans, and they were traded to them. It took the men and two young Monacan friends four and a half months to find those girls. They had been treated harshly and used as slaves. They had almost starved to death by the time their father, and three brothers, and the two young Monacan men discovered them. The girls were tied up in a lean-to, and one of the family's Indian friends slid on his belly during the late of night, cut a slit in the back of the shelter, and silently took the girls out. When morning came, the Indians found they were missing, and they were mad as hell, because those white men made those braves look stupid, so they gathered all together and quickly followed their tracks. The caught up with them before they got to the mountain range they called home. There was a great fight between the Logans, my family, and the two brothers from the Monacan family. Our family prevailed. The two young Monacan Indian men that were our friends, with the aid of our family, killed every one of them. They made it home to a wonderful celebration with all the kin and their blood brothers, the Monacan family.

"I guess it was the watching of the heroics of the two young men that impressed and melted the hearts of the two young girls. The two young men were welcomed to become part of our family. There was some questionable talk with the older men and women, but after the family meeting, they decided it was better to be a family united than a family divided. Now, like every young married couple, the family all helped build the cabins, and let them grow just as they did in the past and continued the tradition on through the years. The youngest girl was fourteen, and her name was Kathryn, and she married the younger of the two brave brothers of the Monacan family, whose name when interpreted was "Hungry Fox," and the family called him "Fox." The other sister, Constance, was sixteen, and she married the older brother who was named "Fast River Otter," but the family called him "Thomas." They decided to take the last name of the girl's mother's maiden name, which was Cook. It seemed no one of the clan could pronounce the tribal names for the young men, so they went along with the family's names. It is all written there in the family Bible." Ida Mae then added that she had a grandson named Fox. We all thought that was pretty cool.

The Monacan ceremonies always took place in the mornings at the rising of the sun, and they feasted all day. The girl's Father, Michael Quinn Cook, gave his daughters away on their special day. The Christian weddings took place in the afternoon, up in the high meadow under the shadow of the pines, in the years of 1720 and 1722.

The marriage of the two girls to the young Monacan men was the first marriage for one hundred years outside of the five families. Within three families, and the Monacans, they brought forth enough children for everyone to marry without looking anywhere else for a mate.

Ida Mae proudly spoke up during this storytelling and said, "With the blending of Indian blood and good Irish/Scots blood, honey, I'm telling you, they made beautiful babies."

She stopped talking a few minutes, laid the book she had held to her breast down, and looked to see who was listening. We all were, of course. How could one not listen? It was quiet, except for that cardinal's message occasionally, and the sounds of the recording equipment. Suddenly, she broke the spell and almost made me jump.

"Well, I want another glass of tea. How about you young folks? Does anybody want any pound cake?"

Marilyn Campbell from Huntington said, "Ida Mae, you just sit still, and I will get the cake and dishes and forks, and I will serve everybody if that's ok with you?"

Ida Mae looked at her and smiled and said, "Sugar, you just go right on and do it your way, and the napkins are in the cabinet beside the ice box. Your momma raised you right."

I sat back and leaned against the walls of the house and let the sun hit me right in the face as I took another drink of that satisfying tea, I closed my eyes and thought of Indians.

✶✶✶✶✶Chapter VI✶✶✶✶✶
Momma and Daddy

P lease tell us about your parents Ida Mae," Jennifer Cline spoke up; the name tag said, History Major from Marshall University in Huntington West Virginia.

Why didn't I think of asking that question? *Shoot!*

Ida Mae placed her hands on her knees and leaned forward with a little squint, and she said slowly, "Well, let's see, I will tell you how they met." She continued with her hypnosis.

It was in the later part of 1850's when Ida Mae's momma was riding with Moses Jewell, Ida Mae's granddaddy, through the woods, along the narrow path following the ridge of old Slip Creek hollow. They came upon the encampment of some hunters. They had two deer hung and gutted and skinned. Mose got fighting mad and told those rascals to leave the mountain that very minute. Well, those men didn't take too kindly to some stranger telling them to get out, just when they were having a good time. Ida Mae's granddaddy was outnumbered by five men. They all stood up, and when it looked like Mose was going to get killed, a couple of men of the Cook and Jewell family rode up with some of the Meade cousins. The hunters saw how big and rowdy those boys looked, and saw that they were all on Mose's side of the argument. The intruders immediately started packing up to leave. Mose and the boys told them not to pack up a thing and to take off all their clothes except their long-johns. He let them know in no uncertain terms that they came to rob the mountain, so they would get robbed themselves.

He ordered them to start walking and be glad that he let them live, and to thank their lucky stars they didn't run into the women folk hunting over on the next ridge because they wouldn't have been so merciful. The strangers had to leave everything they brought up there, including their horses, guns, deer hides and meat, and even had to give up their dogs. The men were boiling mad and threatened to get even. Ida Mae's granddaddy told them if they thought of returning, they wouldn't see their families again, and the rest of our clan would hunt down their families and kill every last one of them. I think the coldness of Mose's black eyes revealed them he was not fooling. They believed him. He said it was no accident that they were caught, the family patrolled the mountain every day. So, if they decided to return, it would not be a happy trip. They walked quickly off to the flatlands and never returned.

After the family had a good laugh and was riding back up the mountain, one of the Cook boys noticed Ida Mae's momma sitting behind her granddaddy Jewell. Her name was Rosebud. He asked Mose, since they were all dividing the spoils of their adventure, could he have his daughter. Rosebud's daddy told him that she was more valuable than all the treasures of Heaven. The brave young boy was named Jacob Thomas Cook. Everybody called him "big Jake" because even when he was a teen, he was taller than his father. The Granddaddy's name was Moses Jewell, but everyone called him "Old Mose."

A week had not passed when Jacob Thomas Cook came calling on Rosebud. 'Jake' Cook was there almost every day and had supper with the family. Rosebud was only thirteen, but she was as tall as a pine and lean as a willow. He hounded Rosebud's daddy for about two years until he finally gave in and allowed them to marry. Yes, they were cousins, but not close ken cousins. It was very common for them not to see some of their cousins for a couple of years. They were pretty spread out. There were so many, and all were busy as an ant colony in different places on the plateau and adjoining ridges, it was hard to have everyone in one place at one time.

After she told us this delightful and enlightening story, she sat back and nodded her head as if she confirmed every word she had just shared.

A voice spoke and said, "Mrs. Cook, why did they call this place Slip

Creek?" It was Cassie Stillwell, from Abingdon, Virginia.

"Well," she said as she thought about the question, "...it seems that when they were trying to get all their stuff up here on the mountain, they followed a mountain stream and had to cross it a couple of times. They said that the rocks were so slick from the green moss that no one could cross the stream without falling into the creek. So, 'Slip Creek' was the only obvious name that came out of it. I know the stream is still dangerous with its moss-covered stones. We all used to fish up there, and every one of us would come home wet because of those blasted slippery rocks." She smiled as she told this story, and we got a kick out of it ourselves.

"Tell us how it was for your parents, and how it was to be little growing up here." Chimed a cute girl from a college in or near Bristol, Virginia, I think.

Ida Mae took another big breath and thought just a minute. Again, she looked upward to think back and see in her mind the story she was about to tell.

Traditions new and old...

I leaned closer in her direction to catch every word. She started out saying that during those days, when her momma and daddy got married, there was still an age-old tradition practiced at that time. When a couple wanted to get married, the families got together and planned the wedding. Of course, we know there are many preachers around now, but back then, preachers were hard to come by, and circuit preachers didn't know the families were up here. So, the couple made their own Christian ceremony. Coming from strong religious backgrounds, they still had strong beliefs. They read from the Bible, and everyone there had a special prayer meeting, some singing, and the couple swore before God and the families that they would honor the ways of the Lord and the code of the clans. They kissed, and then kissed their parents. Then they signed their names in the family bible. A week before the wedding, the boys had cleared off some of the land that the families together had given to the young couple. Every family up here would contribute time and gifts. The men would bring up axes, ropes, hammers, and other things up to the building, and start cutting the right trees for the cabin. They used their mules and workhorses to pull the long logs out of the woods from the other mountain, as they drug the cut timber, they would make a smooth road to the cabin.

There was always a "water witch" in one family or another who could find the right place to dig the well. Ida Mae said there were many springs, as well as natural wet weather springs. It was not hard to find water up there; it was discovering the nearest water source that was the real need. They also dug an outhouse down below the cabin, and away from the main water feed, lined it with stones, put in some lime, and they made it deep to last a long time. While the menfolk were building, the women folk would all take turns in preparing the meals and sending it up where they were working, and sometimes, they would cook right there on the grounds. Some of the close kin with brothers or sisters would camp there in old wagons so they could have an early breakfast and start on the chores of the day.

It wasn't all work; it was a happy time for them all. Everyone assisted in making long tables with some of the split wood, and used logs as their seats, and then they feasted. After all the work of the day was over, and everyone had eaten their fill, they would sit around a good fire and talk of the hard labor and plan the next day's work. There were shingles to be cut and shaved, as well as chinking to be made and then neatly pushed in between the logs. They would be tired, but still loved to get together around the bonfire to tell stories, sing, pray, and talk. When all the work was finished, it was time for the wedding and the big celebration. The families would all gather for the special event. The marriage was performed, and the families would bring an array of many gifts. The gifts were mainly anything to start housekeeping. The usual gifts given were a bred cow, a young bullock, a bred sow, a mule, a little bunch of chickens, a plow, sacks of feed, grain, corn, and a couple of bags of salt, spices, and boxes of tea. If they were lucky, a bag of flour, and salted side meat. Other clan members would bring pieces of homemade furniture, brooms, tools, dishes, cups, skins, and even help plow the fields. While all the men were building the cabin, the women folk after they had the supper cooking, would quilt a blanket for the marriage bed. Sometimes, if they worked well together, a couple of quilts and pillows would be made for the new couple. Usually, the bride's family would make the feather ticking for the bed. It was the biggest celebration that they would have up on the mountain.

The Indian families that lived on the land helped greatly in the celebration. Ida Mae said they were all like family, anyway. They usually helped plow the fields for the corn or even planted it if it was the planting season. The actual wedding and religious ceremony were right in front of the cabin. Wildflowers were picked and put in Rosebud's hair, and she wore her mother's prettiest homemade dress. They said she was the beauty of the Blue Ridge. Her hair hung past her hips and was as black as inside a coal mine, and her eyes were as green as the creek moss they named this place after. Her skin was as fair as a spring lily, and her laughter was contagious. Jake loved her and held her in highest respect all the rest of their days together. He was such a cantankerous old rascal and ruled the roost, but when it came to Rosebud, he was as humble as a little kitten. But he could be a hell-raiser and was the ruler of his kingdom, only because Ida Mae's mother let him. They were such a perfect pair. If you look above Ida's front door, their names are carved there. 'Jacob and Rosebud' with a heart.

Ida Mae said it was another unsaid rule, that after the marriage ceremony, everyone left the young couple alone for about three months, after that, they were expected to try at least to go to family preaching and singing. Celebrations came up when there were good hunting and farming seasons, Christmas, babies being born, and couples getting married, and some getting saved. No one ever visited the newlyweds the first year, unless they were invited. The young couple had to learn to be with each other and learn each other's likes and dislikes without anyone interfering. The same family tradition continued with Ida Mae and her husband. They all seemed to like it that way. In-laws or close friends never butted into any married couple's lives. Being nosey or curious about the new in-laws, was frowned upon and would soon be taken care of by the elders of the family.

Rosebud and Jacob lived up here alone for about three months, and Rosebud said that every time they went to a family gathering or funeral down the road, the women would look at her tummy to see if she was with child. Rosebud was embarrassed to death, and she wouldn't go anywhere for a long time. It was after the first year that Rosebud finally became pregnant, and her momma, seven sisters, and sixteen aunts from both sides of the family, and two older Indian women all gathered together and gave her a celebration. It was just them, but when they all got into a cabin, it was full. The smell of ham biscuits, apple butter, and hot coffee filled the cabin. They told Rosebud stories of birthing and what to do when the time comes, and what to do after the baby arrived, and how to handle the baby and to keep it free from illness. They brought good luck charms, and sweet little gowns and blankets that they had sewn by hand. They brought herbs to be planted such as fever-few and catnip and other herbs used for medicine. Families from both sides were so happy, and soon a handmade cradle and high chair were among the presents given, as well as a beautiful rocking chair that Jacob made for his Rosebud.

Cabin of love and growth

Rosebud had an uncomplicated birth, and the experience of the first baby made her a natural for motherhood. Soon, the babies came about every two or three years or so, until Rosebud was close to forty-five years old. She soon became one of the tellers of stories to young expectant family members. She was also a midwife for many years.

Jake and Rosebud's household glowed and ringed with laughter, love, and children. She was a great cook, and she could hand sew anything. Her kitchen was spotless, and the floors and tables were scrubbed every morning. Her laundry was done twice a week, and she baked some sort kind of bread every day. She was always busy with cooking, canning, or putting up meat, or something going on with the children. Jake could make or build anything, and was always busy, but stayed out of the way. Ida Mae was the middle child of nine children. She had six brothers and two sisters.

During this time, there were settlements and townships around the river valley, and some of the menfolk traded at some of the trading posts for gossip, coffee, flour, and salt. For the first time, buying goods wasn't such a hard task as the trips in the past sometimes would take two days. Jake took advantage of the new businesses, as he would find a card game or a cock-fight to bet on about once a week. Jake had a natural business mind. He was never without a five-dollar gold piece in his pocket when at that time, a lot of the mountain people had never seen a gold coin. He loved to gamble, and did so often enough down on the river or over into the next county. He raced horses, and bought and sold them as well; he kept a grand kennel with hunting dogs that he sold and traded often. He also had fightin' roosters, and he made the best moonshine in the whole country. Ida Mae's daddy even preached a couple of times. Whatever was needed, he was there to fill the need, if there was a dollar in the plan. He would never let people come to the house to trade. He always took his wares down to the river where he did his business. A couple of his brothers or cousins would go with him, in case he might meet up with a low lander who wanted to rob him. They stopped many a would-be- thief. Jake wasn't all business; he would also play with the kids in the meadows and the barns until Momma Rosebud called them in to eat. She would sometimes scold him for acting like a child, and he would just look at them and smile that silly little half-cocked smile of his, and the kids would bust out laughing so loud and then Momma Rosebud would laugh at the thought of changing him. Ida Mae said it in a nutshell, "Lordy, they loved each other so much."

Ida Mae shifted herself in her chair and took another sip of tea and took her handkerchief and wiped her neck and forehead. She took a few deep breaths and crossed her legs and picked up another journal, then started talking more about her childhood.

She said that they didn't have much of a yard to play in because her dad thought it would be a waste of land to have a yard when the kitchen garden could be more significant. All the kitchen or cooking herbs were planted there, along with rows of ginseng planted on the shady side. His reason for planting the kitchen garden so close to the kitchen door was because Momma Rosebud always had a young'in on her hip and she didn't need to be too far from the house to gather what she needed. It was handier for her to walk out from the side kitchen door and step into a full kitchen garden for her needs. The kids didn't need a play yard, as they had meadows, barns, orchards, and mountains along with waterfalls and streams to play in every day. The children didn't have a regular pet when they were little, mostly because their daddy said that he did not want anything here at the farm that didn't pay its way. He said if he couldn't eat it, work it, fight it, milk it, breed it, trade it, sell it, hunt it, bet on it, or ride it, it didn't belong there.

"Daddy Jake" would go what they called "sangin," that's ginseng digging, every spring, and bring a poke full of fresh dug up plants and replanted them in the garden and other places close to the house. He taught them to never take all of the plants. They always left some, especially if they had berries on them. So, the garden stayed, and got bigger and bigger down through the years. He explained to his children that they had the woods and meadows to romp and play in all day. I guess he was right. He did not want anything or anyone to be wasteful. So, if they got a hankerin' to pet or play with a dog, they had to play with "Daddy Jake's" hunting hounds and some of their pups. There were always new pups to train, or new little pigs, or baby chicks, or even baby goats and calves. Daddy Jake wouldn't let them tame or play with any wild critters. It was a strict rule, and they were all made to understand the wild had to stay wild. They had horses to ride whenever they wanted; it seemed Ida Mae was the one who loved horses. It just came naturally for her to be around horses and to ride better than all her brothers and sisters. They had a wonderland to play in, and had their choice of things to play with; they just couldn't get too attached to things. Later, Ida Mae ended up with a walker-pup that her daddy gave her, only because she showed interest in the hunting dogs. "Daddy Jake" said she had a keen eye for dog flesh. Maybe, it was because he favored Ida Mae, as she was more like him than the other children.

Rich in love, laughter, and family

Ida Mae looked us over and said, "I guess by your standards today, we would have been considered poor. But, we didn't know that at the time. We thought we were rich and lived in paradise. It just got lonely sometimes. There was always hot food on the table and plenty put back in the side house, we had meat hanging in the smokehouse, canned vegetables, and the potato mound was always full, and so was the spring house. We didn't get new clothes that often, but we didn't miss that. We got shoes in the fall and had a good coat. We didn't know the difference between rich and poor."

When Ida Mae spoke, her voice and demeanor seemed almost holy. I would get goosebumps when she talked about her daddy and momma.

She smiled and said, "I had the best daddy. He loved his babies, and he made sure there was plenty of laughter. I swear, he could turn a dollar faster than any person I ever knew. He never went off the mountain without returning home with 'folding money' in his pocket. He never came home empty-handed. There was never a turkey shoot that my daddy didn't win, or at least get a second place prize. He was always bringing home a beef steer or a sow with little ones, or he would win some bet and bring home a mule that he would later trade for cash or for some other critter that he could use to make a fast dollar. He would bring in huge bags of flour, bags of sugar, and coffee. Like I told you before, we had great hunting dogs and the bloodline was sought by every coon and bear hunter along the river. We bred those good hounds for as long as I can remember. I am proud to say that three Governors owned some of my daddy's pups. My sons still have the same bloodline and trades, and sell just like their granddaddy did."

Ida Mae did love her daddy, and as she spoke, she had to smile with a tender tear, as she reminisced those golden days of childhood. When I thought back about mine, I felt cheated. If I had only been born up in the mountains somewhere, like her and her family, and had the wilderness as my playground, I would have been such a satisfied child. The day before I had ever met Ida Mae, I never in a million years would have thought such a thing.

Ida Mae continued to talk about her daddy and her momma, and the stories kept flowing from her, placing a joy in all our hearts and minds. As she said, her daddy was industrious, and they never did without. He was an excellent wood worker and made wooden toys, dough bowls, tables, chairs, and moonshine, which didn't have a thing to do with toys, but he used the scrap wood for the fire to boil the shine. Rosebud hated him making corn liquor. When he would come home after working up at the still, he would have to sleep on the porch, or back in the back room. He would have a terrible smell of sweat, wood smoke, and burnt sugar on his body and clothing. Rosebud would fuss all day, but he would stroll on up to the still while she would be shouting at him from the porch. She didn't fuss too much at him come Christmas time, when they had more than enough food in the pantry, or when he would go into to town to sell and come back home with new clothing for them all, bolts of material and thread, along with new shoes. Ida May said her momma used her anger at convenient times. She would calm down and give him peace when she thought he was making good money.

Ida Mae said, with some pride in her voice, "He and his twelve brothers were the best 'shine makers in a three-hundred-mile radius. After the corn was up and harvested, and then worked down, that's when the 'shine' would pour. Most of the men from down at the trading stores would gather on the river road the first of the month in October to buy Daddy's shine, and the first of every month after that for a while. There had been many a night that Daddy didn't come home because they worked all night filling hundreds of jugs. Those filled jugs made the family extra money that kept us and this old farm prosperous for many a year."

She turned and looked out over the railings of the porch into the lovely climbing rose vine, as it seemed she was looking into Heaven. She then turned her eyes to the house; I know now, she had a vision of her mother standing there on that porch, remembering the beauty she was. I could see it on her face and in her eyes.

She finally spoke and said, "Our mommy was a beauty. She had long fingers and could play the fiddle with the best of the men. She loved those Irish tunes that her grandfather taught her. She taught all her children to play music. I loved to play the guitar as she played the old fiddle, and my brother, Elbert, played the banjo, and my other brother Daniel played a small type of guitar. My two sisters had wonderful voices and were not shy to sing in front of the family. The other cousins would come by on a Friday afternoon and stay and bring their instruments, and we would play music all weekend. Momma would only stop to put in a large pan of biscuits and fry up some side meat and make a strong pot of coffee. She always had a stack cake or something sweet during the weekends. The women folk who didn't play or sing, would clean the house and cook other things like apple pies and keep the coffee poured, and the dishes and cups washed. Our house was full of family love, and was warm in the winter and smelled of aged wood smoke and bacon. I love that smell to this day. Oh, my goodness, those were such wonderful days."

It was time to take another break, and I could tell Ida Mae needed one as well. We all moved around and stretched a little bit. We chatted about school and our plans after we graduated, and what kind of jobs we would like to have, and our dreams and wishes. But after about ten minutes or so, we were ready to get back to the story of Ida Mae Cook's life.

...And also, every man should eat and drink, and enjoy
all the good of his labour, it is the gift of God.

Ecclesiastes 3:13 King James Version (KJV)

Chapter VII

Growth in Space and in Wisdom

We got our second wind, and so did our gracious host. Our batteries were changed and checked, our pens were ready, the pages turned to the new ones, and we were more than ready.

She said that she wanted to talk about the cabin.

She told us, "Daddy built on the cabin all the time, and had plans drawn on brown paper that Momma folded and put in the kitchen ceiling in the rafters. Daddy would take it down occasionally, and bring the lamp over on the kitchen table, and look at it and add a thing or two, fold it back up and stick it back in the same spot."

She went on with the story about her daddy and the cabin's grown through the years. She said that her daddy would add a room to the house about every five years or so, and constantly worked on the ever-growing foundation, and he was always bringing in large rocks. He and his cousins rolled three cabins, using ropes, logs, and work horses to move them. He added them to the main house, and cut out the walls and joined them expertly. Even in those years, the house seemed large, but it must have been full of family. If a family decided to move from their cabin, her dad and the boys would relocate the cabins, either to add to the main house or to be closer, for one reason or the other. If there were family members who were sick or just getting older, there was a cabin waiting for them, fully furnished.

She had a few photos of the family standing in front of the main cabin before it grew. The original cabin seemed small for the number of children that lived there. She told us about the ongoing work on the cabin that kept everybody busy. They always took care of the older family members, which we all thought was admirable.

The good life that they had up here, it's no wonder they lived long. She said that the elders of the family were the grandparents or even great-grand parents of that family. They lived close by, and when they got older, all lived together. The families held their elderly in the highest esteem, and they were so honored and asked for their wisdom for problem-solving. They came in handy come planting time, and they would watch the little ones and kept them out of harm's way and kept them fed and happy. The elders are not shuffled off to some old folk's home where no one knows where they are or cares. That doesn't happen up here. Their opinions mean something, and they are useful and productive until the day they die. She laughed when she said, "Guess that's why I lived so long, I was needed. Thank God."

She stopped talking and then you could see a thought come to her. "Jenny," she called to her daughter who was still sitting in the kitchen, listening to the stories.

Jenny answered," What is it, Momma?"

"Bring me the pictures on the mantle. I want to show them the pictures of my children." She sounded just like some proud grandmother wanting her company to see the pictures. Jenny was at least seventy-five or eighty, and she moved very well for her age. She brought out about eight picture frames and laid them on Ida Mae's lap.

She held up the first one and said, "This here is a picture of Jenny, she's the one in the kitchen. Here's her family of five children. They're all grown and live in Charlotte, Roanoke, and in Lexington. Jenny married Albert Arms from the bottom land, but he died in the mines. That's him in this picture with her when they were young. Jenny had a twin brother, but he died a week after they were born. He couldn't breathe very well, and it made him just too weak to live. I don't have a picture of him, but I remember his beautiful little body as if it were last week.

"This here is my son Jacob, named after his grandfather, with his family.

56

He lives down across the next holler with his wife, Earlene. They had seven children and twenty-one grandchildren, and they all live either with him or very near. He has a bigger farm than I do."

She passed out the framed pictures as if handing out playing cards. We all crowded around her.

"This here is a picture of my son Brown and his family. His wife's name is Carrie Ann, and she is from a different holler than here. They had eight children, and they have thirteen grandchildren. I almost lost Brown with a high fever when he was just a baby."

She continued to tell us that a disease hit the mountain and the low land people very hard in the early twentieth century. It was called the Spanish Influenza, and many people died during that terrible outbreak. "Most of the children on the mountain were spared, thank God. We paid a hefty price for being God's favorites."

We held and passed the pictures around. "Here is a picture of Elbert, and Daniel; I named them after my brothers. They all moved away from the home place, but live just down the road a little piece, on their own land. They have big families too. The other picture here is my baby girl, her name was Kathryn, and she died of cancer. She was only thirty years old when she died. She had three children that I, along with her husband Buford, raised. I made them move in with me so we all could help. Their children are all up and grown and have grown children of their own. Their oldest boy is a doctor in Charlottesville Virginia, at the University Hospital. The youngest girl went on with her education, and teaches there at the University of Virginia, and the youngest boy is a lawyer in Washington D.C. Every one of those children grew up to be respectable adults, and well educated too. Their daddy, Buford, died last year of a heart attack, it was quick and painless, I believe, but it was God's will. Not for us to question. Della is my adopted daughter, she lives over in War with her husband, Sheb Hatfield. Larence, my first adopted child, was a federal mine inspector and he lives in Pineville along with his wife, Leeta. I got him when he was two. His parents were my cousins, and they were killed in a car crash down in Welch. Lawrence and Leeta have five grown children. Carson, my red-headed son, is married and lives over in Bradshaw, he has three children. He lives just a few miles as the crow flies, and he drove a coal truck for JM&T Coal Company for twenty years, he still preaches on Sundays. He isn't well, and I worry about him all the time. This picture is of my sweetie pie, Nathan. His precious mother, who was my second cousin, died hours after giving birth to him, and his father gave him to me. I took him in when he was only twenty-four hours old. He lives the closest to me, just next door. He is retired from the school, and works this farm with his five sons, whom are all married and have children. He comes to see me every day, and his kids check on my needs all the time."

She bowed her head and took a few deep breaths. We were quiet and watched her as she rocked back and forth a couple of times, and seemed she was regaining her strength for the next story. I could tell she dreaded talking about this part of this conversation.

"I tell you all this, young people, you will never know such pain or loss until you bury one of your babies. A loving parent should not out live their babies. God has all the answers. I just figured that all of us are on loan here, and when your time is through, you must go."

She looked around like a good teacher would, and got eye contact before she spoke again. "You just play the hand that is dealt, and you either continue to play or fold and quit, and I'll be hanged if I'll fold. You can believe that!"

Three of us gathered the pictures up, and I took them into the house and laid them on the coffee table in front of the sofa. Ida Mae stopped and was quiet. She got up and went into the house. We all looked around at each other and with questions in our minds; did it get too deep for her and did her emotions and memories get the best of her? Did she get tired or did she quit; or would she come back? We waited, and I heard her blow her nose and mumble something to Jenny, and she then hollered upstairs to someone unseen, "You all open up that back-bedroom window and let that room air out." A muffled answer of, "Okay Maw" was all we heard. Just a few minutes had passed, and Ida Mae came back out on the porch. She looked refreshed. We all were relieved to know that she was going to resume.

I asked her if she was tired, and she said, "Yes, honey, I am tired, but not because of you fine young people, I had to check to see if my household was in order. I just can't let them do things on their own without me guiding them. It is my house, you know."

She smiled and fluffed her pillows before sitting down. I could tell she loved to rock in that white rocking chair. It made a creaking noise as she rocked back and forth. Suddenly, as if on cue, there was the most perfect breeze blowing around the cabin, and the hummingbirds were having to work extra hard to maintain an even flying pattern while trying to get to those beautiful, red blossoms planted in a lard bucket at the other end of the porch. The flowering bushes all around the front of the road and the edges of her yard drew every butterfly and bumble bee for miles. Her porch received the sweet smell of every blossom, and we all breathed it in deeply, to enjoy the essences of Ida's mountain paradise. It was intoxicating.

She spoke up without being prompted and said, "My daddy made this here rocking chair, and every chair on this porch. Now this old chair creeks and it sounds like my old bones. He made every stick of wooden furniture that is in my house, and a dozen or so cabins on over the hill. Like I said, my daddy could make anything. He made the cradle that I put my babies in, and made many of the toys they played with and cut their teeth on."

One of the many things she said that was notable, was about remembrance of her childhood. She said that her early years were blessed, and she didn't know that they did without the finer things of life. She thought they did have the finer things as they would play tag in the meadow, and in the woods, swing from a grapevine, or chase little pigs and chickens. The family started the morning before the sun rose, and finished their day when the sun went down. It was the nature of all things. When it was dark, they slept, and when there was light, they awoke. Simple as that.

Everyone up on the mountain had to start their chores early, and even little Ida Mae had her jobs. She got to feed the chickens, and her daddy built a small wagon and put a feed bucket in it. Little Ida Mae pulled it into the chicken coop where she fed the chickens every day. She said she never was pecked or flogged by an angry hen or rooster. Guess they knew right away that she was Jake's baby, and they would be on the dinner table come Sunday afternoon if they laid as much as a feather on her. Ida Mae said that she remembered that her daddy was over-protective of his babies. One of the times when she was out feeding the chickens, and a big dog tried to get into the coop, and she tried to block him with her little body; the dog knocked her down and gave a vicious growl. Her daddy appeared from out of nowhere. He choked the dog to death in front of her and the whole barnyard. He took it away in the woods. I guess the animal kingdom got the message. Nothing ever raised a hoof, claw, or feather, or showed a tooth in her direction again.

Her dad did teach them many things about the mountain ways, especially about being responsible thinkers. They had berry picking rules, such as always stay together, and never pick all the berries, and never fail to take a couple of hounds with you. He told them to never stomp on the berry plants and be gentle when picking. That's the way he thought about digging ginseng. He would take the large roots and never touch a berry, and if some fell off, he would plant it. By doing this, he made sure that it would continue to grow and produce. He knew where all the patches of ginseng, or "sang" as he called it, were grown. Like Ida Mae said before, he was always in the money business. They still have ginseng up here from the original plantings.

Ida Mae continued with her historical saga and smiled while thinking what she was going to say next. She remembered a time when all the children went to a special place in the early spring. They called it "Strawberry Hill," and they would go there to pick the new berries. She said it was a small knoll that would turn bright red in the early spring, and if they could get there before the animals, they would bring a bountiful harvest. Always leave some berries so they could go to seed and also to feed the other animals. The main berry hunting rule was that they were never to go out alone. They had to take the hounds because bears love berries, and the hounds would send the bears running back off the mountain.

I had to smile thinking about running in those hills with buckets and gathering such a sweet, little mouth full. Her stories took us all to another place that only our imaginations could travel.

"After all the berry and apple picking," she continued, "Momma would make the best strawberry jam and apple butter you could ever slap on a biscuit. She would work outside in the big copper kettle over a fire. Using a long wooden paddle that was made years before she was born, she stirred while it would boil and added the sugar and other stuff to it 'til she was satisfied. Only she knew when it was ready to fill the jars. The kids had to stay clear of the fire and the pot. She was extremely watchful because she was burned as a child with hot apple butter. She carried the scars on her legs to the grave. Momma would fill close to a hundred or more jars of jams and jellies, and we waited 'til they cooled to take them down to the cellar to keep until winter. Many other jars would be in the pantry inside the house, to use 'til we needed the others. Now that I think about it, I do believe that during the summertime we were the busiest. But, it meant having something extra on the table during the winter. With such a large family, we had to work hard to make sure we were all happy all through the year. We never heard of the event or the word 'vacation.'"

Ida Mae and her siblings thought that summer was the most fun of all, and the busiest. The learning of survival happened in the summer. After all the work with the strawberries, a month later they were busy blackberry picking, raspberry picking, and then there were chickapins, walnuts, hickory nuts, and chestnuts, and then they were busy doing some of the field's harvest. The apple and pear season seemed to be the hardest and the longest. The families had at one time at least fifty apple trees and twenty pear trees in the orchard, about ten cherry trees, chestnut trees, and walnut trees grew all over. They all worked and peeled and cooked apples and pears for weeks. They dried fruit all summer. The women stretched out oilcloth, and dried apples and pears on the roof of the cabin. Of course, "Daddy Jake" had to have some for his apple doin's. He made what they called hard apple cider or Apple Jack; he called it apple "squeezin'." There was a good market for that too. Everyone put up bushels of winter apples wrapped in straw filled boxes in the spring house.

After another break, she opened up and gathered her class in and said, "I loved going into the spring house, as it was dark and so cool. Ours was more extensive than most spring houses. It had to be. My great-grandfather built it out of stone that he proudly dug out when planning the spring house. Most of the spring house is under ground. He dug it out and constructed it back into a hill, or what we call a bank. The spring was the sweetest, most refreshing water anyone ever drank, and still runs freely there, keeping the spring house unique of all the buildings, and a very desirable spot to lie down on the cool stone during an August blast of summer. While we were just about to get into the cherry season, June apples came into season, and we would switch around picking duties so we would not get bored at one job. That was so much fun. We climbed trees like squirrels and fought those pesky blue jays for the best of the crop. I guess we put up as many cherries as we did strawberries. The kettle was brought back out, cleaned, and put into use again. Raspberry season is short, as well as blackberry season, and the hustle to get them all picked before the birds got them was hard. Just when we thought there would be a lull in the canning, the garden was up, and we canned everything. Hundreds of jars of beans, pickles, canned meat, and fruit."

She got up, went inside and came back out with a large jar of honey. It was almost clear with a slight amber glow. Turning the jar as to let the bubble inside slowly slide up the inside of the jar, she told us because it was so rich and thick, it was the best honey they ever harvested from their hives. Ida Mae said, "Our honey never turns to sugar. Our bees have so many blossoms from the clover and fruit trees to make this honey; there isn't any need for anything else. We use a lot of honey for our sweetnin' and our molasses, and not so much sugar. We think its just healthier.

"Years ago while my grandparents were here, they reaped the benefits of having the blossoms in the spring and the blooming of the meadow, their honeybees were very productive. Honey flowed like water and was so pure and sweet. It still is! Just like the Bible talked about, our land flowed with milk and honey and surely was the 'Promised Land.'

"Just like those old Indians said about the mountain providing everything for us, just about every need we had was met. We did eat and live well."

Not all was fun and games...

Although summer was a lot of work and fun, there was one incident that Ida Mae talked a little more about the berry business. It all sounded so much fun, but she added to the storytelling about the dangers of the mountain as well. She said that in midsummer, all the cousins of every family would bring pull wagons and every pot, bucket, or anything that would hold the blackberries, raspberries, huckleberries, and wild blueberries. Now, this was the time that Ida Mae mentioned before that they had to have the hounds, because it was also very hazardous for the kids to be out in tall grass and thickets because of the copperhead snakes and the rattlers. The rattlesnakes would at least give you a fair warning with their rattles, but the copperheads would lay in wait on you and get you if you were not paying attention. Their old mule came in real handy during those times. Not only did the mule give the weary children a ride back home, but she said that mule would stomp the life out of any snakes around. I guess that was the reason why her daddy didn't get mad if they took the old mule with them out from the house. The hounds would be the first into the bushes and the grasses. They pulled out many a snake that would have bitten them.

One story that she remembered and told us was one spring morning after the fog had lifted, Ida Mae and her brothers and sisters took their baskets and buckets, and with the aid of one of Jake's work mules and his short wagon, they all left out to pick strawberries. They had to take Bugle with them and old 'Knot Head' too. She said with a smile that those were the best dogs a kid could have around, and her daddy said they were the best coonhounds he had ever had. They went to the strawberry hill as they did every year, only this year was extremely hot for early spring, and they were already tired before they were halfway through. The strawberries were the sweetest they had been in years, and the mountain was just full of them. Ida spied a bright red patch, just below the old chestnut that lightning had struck, and she took her basket down there. Old Bugle and Knot Head had followed her as usual, and she had just laid a basket down when she heard that dreaded sound of a rattler. She froze and didn't move a muscle until old Bugle came and stood between the snake and Ida Mae. Knot Head pushed her back with his body and knocked her down. The snake struck old Bugle on his left hip. Just then, that work mule who had been grazing close to her came over and stomped that snake to death. She said that she hugged and kissed that old mule. The mule and the dogs had saved her life.

They had filled all the baskets and buckets anyway, so they loaded up the wagon and put Bugle in the back. Jake knew something had happened because the kids had come home early, and he ran out of the barn to see what was the matter. When he saw old Bugle in the back of the wagon, he knew that he had been snake bit. The kids told him all the details. Jake picked the dog up and took him to the barn. He told them all to stay away and Ida figured he was going to kill him. Jake didn't come back until late that night, and he had worked on old Bugle and put some kind of poultice on his bite. Bugle lay in the hay for about three days and finally came out much thinner, but alive. Knot Head never left his side. That sweet work mule got extra feed for a month, and old Knot Head and Bugle got some meaty bones as well.

The motivation of all the work and struggles was the thought of the Harvest Celebration, which later became Thanksgiving and Christmas. I can only dream of the smells in that kitchen, in the dead of winter, of apple cakes, berry cobblers, roasted chestnuts, hot cider, meats and vegetables roasting, and homemade breads. The sounds in the house during that time were probably ringing sounds of excited laughter and a sweet fiddle playing an Irish reel. These were simpler times, but Ida Mae's people were not simple people. They were brilliant.

Food preservation was not the only thing the family did to stay busy, but there were also other necessities that had to be met. They made the soap that they used for everything. The women folk got together in the spring and the fall and made lye soap two times a year. They made enough soap for everyone. Once again the large kettle was brought back out of the barn, and was used for the soap making; this task took two full days. They took turns stirring using a long, specially made wooden paddle, stirring with long, round sweeps. Ida Mae's daddy and her husband would help pour the mixture into large pans, and they would let it cool during the evening. After it had cooled, they would take a large knife and cut the hardened soap into blocks, some large and some small, for large hands and small hands. They made all the candles too. The women just quit making soap a year ago. She said her soap had other things added to it that her mother didn't add. Ida Mae added oatmeal, and blossoms, and other herbs to make it smell and feel better. Her soap had a sweeter smell than that of her mother's, but it did not smell as perfumey like the soaps you buy today in the supermarkets. Ida Mae said she would put her soap up against any brand for getting dirt off the body, stains out of clothing, and just cleaning up everything. It made the skin feel good too, and when they washed their hair and let it dry in the sun, the shine off their hair would blind you. They never had split ends, and none of the menfolk went bald. She never had bumps on her face. I don't know if that was because of the pure soap, or the pure food. I guess the proof is there. When she finished telling the story, she laughed out loud and slapped her knees, and we all laughed with her.

"Our lives were spent working hard one day so we would have a better day the next. Just like the Bible tells us. We worked and were thankful. After all, God made this paradise just for us. He shared this place us. I have seen proof that God loves this old farm, as the mountain mist rises to the Heavens, and each little bird, or ladybug, or butterfly has a purpose — to please God right here. I have felt the Lord pass by, and I have felt His presence all around here. I believe He comes here to take a pleasant walk when He needs to rest."

It seemed when she said that, I got chills up my spine. Perhaps He was with us, right there on that long porch, as we learned about the special place He had made. The sun was bouncing off her pearl white hair and for an instant, I thought I saw a halo glow around her head.

"You know, we had to plan ahead for every day and every season," she said.

"Just when the time came that we thought we might run out of our jams, jellies, and preserves, it was time to make more and do it all again. We always put up more than we needed. Momma said that we might face drought or late frosts, or whatever Mother Nature decided to do. Momma made sure we were not lacking in anything if she could help it. This is the way they were raised, and it is the way I was raised. Daddy's barn was full of hay, and he had it stacked in the corner of every meadow that we owned. He always had enough for winter feeding, plus he always kept extra feed in the loft in both big barns. We all were pressured to be prepared for anything."

There was a pause. Ida sat back and closed her eyes for a second. We all looked up at her because she had taken a deep breath, and we also took a deep breath. She picked up her glass of tea and saw that the glass was empty. She placed it on the coaster on the table, then tilted her head slightly. She looked so wise and wonderful sitting there. I never thought of an old person like that before in my life. This feeling while watching her felt like the first time I got to go to the Smithsonian, in Washington, D.C.; I was awestruck. She was my first live hero. I didn't want to leave here. Not now anyway. She was a fountain of powerful, meaningful stories. I thought she was the coolest thing since The Rolling Stones. She was real. She didn't know how to lie. She saw history happen. She was history!

She got up and went down the steps of the porch, and walked without assistance to the pump. I jumped up and went behind her to at least help her. She smiled at me as I pumped the fresh water from the red painted pump. Besides, it was fun to work the handle. I had never done that before. I always thought water pumps looked great in those old western movies and on TV shows. She took the long handled tin cup and dipped it into the stream of water. She splashed me a little bit, but I didn't care. She drank the whole cup, then rinsed it out and hung it up on the little hook that was there.

She turned to me and said with a wink, "You know, I have running water in the house now, but it just doesn't taste as good as when you have to go and fetch it."

I looked at her and said that I knew exactly what she was talking about. I did know. I let her put her arm on mine and we walked up the little bank, and up to the steps of the cabin. I felt important, and even blessed just touching her. I felt important because she let me touch her. She put her trust in me to help her. I was honored.

The air was getting warmer but in the shade of those huge trees, it smelled so sweet and so green. That is the only way I can describe it. It just smelled green. On the way back up, she stopped and looked up into the thick, densely leaved trees and smile as if looking at her friend, God. I am sure she sensed something there, and I felt it too. I expected to see angels coming through the pine thicket or across the meadow. It would have been a natural sight.

Chapter VIII

True and Scary Stories as was Told to Us

I da Mae, with all the spooky dark places here, with those deep dark woods around you, did you ever see anything? Do you believe in ghosts? Did you ever get scared up here?"

"Well," she said as she lightly chuckled a little low. "I knew that would be one of the questions you young people would ask," she tossed her head back and laughed out loud. She continued with a smile in her voice.

"Everyone wants to know about old 'hant stories' because everybody knows how dark and strange these mountains are anyway. Now, I'll just tell ya. When we were little, we didn't have Halloween like you do now, going from house to house, getting candy, and pulling pranks and all, Oh, Lord no! We had better." Ida put her hands together in her lap and told this story to us. She said that this story was told to all of them and was handed down.

"The Indians up here and all my relatives told it for as long as I can remember. Back in the early 1800's, there was a rich hunter that came up into this mountain range, just a couple of ridges over, on the back side. He had his dogs and a couple of his hunting friends, and two black servants to help them with the camp and a few hunting dogs. Well, the story goes that the hunting party came upon an Indian hunting party. They met and talked and made peace with one another, and the Indians invited them back to their summer hunting camp down in the valley a ways. Now the Indians from these parts traveled around to follow the elk and the buffalo and the beaver. There was a lot of game here one time, but the family must have chased them out of here with the building of cabins and plowing of fields, and all those hollering children whooping it up all over the place. They scared most of the big game past the Mississippi!"

We all laughed at her because she was laughing so hard, and she slapped her knees with both hands, and she was so animated. Her laughter was so contagious, and we all were laughing with her. It took about five minutes for us all to settle down.

She collected herself, wiped her eyes with a tissue she had tucked in bosom, which took a few minutes, and started again.

"But, back to the story. Those Indians treated those hunters nice and they stayed the night with them. The next morning those black servants woke up early to fix the breakfast, and when they got out of their tent, the whole camp was gone. The white men, the horses, the dogs, and the Indians were just gone. The two black men walked down to the other camp where they were first staying, and nothing was there either. Not even tracks. Those two black men walked all the way back to where they lived and told their stories, and was told they would be hanged for murder. No one believed them, and for all they knew, those two black servants just up and killed the hunters. No one checked out the story. But sometimes during a full moon, you can hear horses running through the woods with a few Indian shouts, and even an old lonely hound baying at the moon. Then you can see the lights of the lanterns going through the woods being carried by the ghosts of the two black men hunting for their masters. All of them up there just hunting."

She said that the reason they were up there hunting was because they were huntin' lost people to take their souls, so they could live again. After she told the story, she added this, "Better believe that when the sun started to go down, honey, you would find us real close to the house."

We all looked at each other and made a silent pact to leave before the sun went down.

We turned our pages and made as little noise as we could, so she would continue and not forget. Someone asked, "Ida Mae do you have another?" I didn't even turn around to see who asked the question.

She answered, "Why, I have a hundred of them, sugar, but I don't have the time or the breath to tell them all, but I do want to tell an extraordinary story, that I know it to be true as told to me by my uncles and aunts. I know where the farm is, and I have seen the old house myself."

She managed to give a little twisted smile and peered into the kitchen to see if her daughter was listening to her. She started where she left off.

"This story was told to all of us, and I honestly believe them. It was about an old woman who lived by herself, just over a couple of ridges adjoining another mountain ridge to this one. Her name was Zetty Hanshoe Mullins. She helped wounded animals, and those wild animals would come of their own free will for her to heal them and feed them. Even deer that had been shot, but not mortally wounded, would come and lay their heads on her lap as she sat on her porch and removed the arrowheads. Hawks and eagles would stay on her back porch, as well as squirrels, groundhogs, skunks, and raccoons, and she would talk to all of them. Old Zetty raised rows and rows of corn, beans, root vegetables, and sugar cane to feed those wild critters, and she would have the best garden of anyone in this country, well maybe the second best. No one had a garden that could compare to my daddy's. Anyhow, the animals would not steal from her garden, because they knew she fed them from it. She fed the animals all her table scraps, and put out hay in the winter for the deer, salt licks, and straw in the back for them to bed down in. Her whole mountainside was just thick with game. We heard tell that one day two hunters came up on the mountain to hunt whitetail deer, and the critters told old Zetty that they were there. One man started to shoot a deer and had it in his sights when suddenly, a big black crow swooped down on his head and knocked him down. While he was getting himself up and picking up his gun, a black bear charged him from behind and that hunter was mauled to death. The other man ran off the mountain and never returned after his buddy's body. Everyone that went up on the mountain with a gun ended up dead. People did visit old Zetty though, and she welcomed them in, but you had to step over squirrels, raccoons, skunks, and a snake or two, but nothing that was there would ever show one bit of mean or growl at you or show one tooth, as long as you came in peace. People that knew her would bring extra stuff from their gardens to help

Zetty feed her 'babies' as she would call them. She loved the big birds of the forest, and she always had a crow or a red-tailed hawk on her shoulder and a ground squirrel in her pocket. Never a talon would scratch her."

She raised her eyebrows and looked over her glasses to see the expression on our faces. I guess she was happy in what she saw in our expressions, as our mouths were open with excitement. She leaned forward as to talk to us personally, and began in a lower voice.

"Well, one summer, Zetty hadn't been seen in town for a couple of weeks when the preacher, the doctor, and the sheriff decided it would be on the safe side to visit her and see if she was okay. They rode their horses up the hill, and it seemed that the horses knew the way. After a few hours of that rough ride, they arrived at the top of the ridge. They tied off their horses and walked up to old Zetty's cabin and knocked on the door, but there wasn't an answer. They heard a scuffle inside, so they opened the door and Zetty was sitting at her table. The sheriff asked her why she didn't answer the door, and she said she was busy.

"He said, 'Busy doing what?'

"She answered, 'I just flew in the window when you knocked at the door.'

"The preacher and the sheriff just looked at each other. The doctor couldn't take his eyes off Zetty. Zetty had a smile on her face and a few black feathers caught in her frazzled, grey hair and a few more on the floor.

"The doctor asked her, 'So you have been flying outside here?'

"Zetty said, 'Why sure Doc, sometimes my old feet just get too tired of walking the same old space, and I just have to take wing and fly with my friends! Why Doc, you ain't seen the mountains proper 'til you see it from up in the air, like the birds.'

"The doctor told her they were just checking on her, and they would be back soon to check on her again. When they got back down the mountain and went into town, Doc called Zetty's cousin, her only living relative, to come into town and they would make arrangements have her committed to the State hospital. Two weeks had passed when Doc and the sheriff traveled back up to bring Zetty down the mountain. When they got there, they went into the cabin and told Zetty that they were taking her to a nice place to live, and that she would never have to worry about anything again. She laughed out loud and told them, 'How can you cage a wild creature of the forest?' Just then, she turned and transformed herself into a doe, and jumped up on the kitchen table and leaped out the open kitchen window. The doctor ran after the doe, and the sheriff ran right behind them. From behind a tree in the distance stood Zetty in her human form, and told them that she was happy right where she lived, and if anyone else came up on the mountain, they would get a big surprise.

"The two men got on their horses and rode quietly down the holler, about halfway down, they saw a mountain lion. The horses didn't bolt or act nervous. The big cat just walked calmly past them and looked over its shoulder, and then blended into the tall grass. The two men knew that they were looking at old Zetty in another form. It was told that Zetty's cousin had a nighttime visitor that had appeared in her hotel room, and after that, she never wanted to help Zetty anymore. No one ever mentioned old Zetty again, and she never went into town. Her cabin is still up the hollow on the other side of this ridge, and the animals still stay around the cabin, and the corn still grows, and the garden spot still produces. The hay fields are still there, and no one messes with a thing. That is why we are kind to all animals up here on this mountain. Lord knows that we don't want to do an unkind thing to any animal because it could be old Zetty in her animal form."

All the students on the porch were quiet, and their eyes were as big as dinner plates.

She looked around and leaned forward and started again. "I have to say, that all the other stories were hand-me-downs. This one story that I am going to tell you, this happened to me when I was a little girl. One time, I had to stay up here with my brothers and sisters for two nights without Momma and Daddy. They had to go to a funeral of a friend down the mountain. Daddy knew that no one would bother us up here, and besides, the older kids would watch out for us little'uns. I had a hound pup that I loved dearly, and it was not allowed in the house. But since Momma and Daddy were not home, I decided that the pup could stay in my bed and keep me company. We all had our supper and did our chores, and it was getting late. The pup started whining at the door, wanting out. My oldest brother told me to let it out and watch it, and when it gets through doing its business, I could let him back in. I opened the door and let the pup out, and he went into the grass and squatted. I stood on the porch in my nightgown waiting, when all the sudden, a large, dark, hairy thing stood up in the grass. I screamed bloody murder, and all my brothers and sisters came running from all corners of this cabin, and the pup ran into the house with his tail between his legs just shivering. We all saw this thing that came walkin' very slowly up to the cabin. We bolted every door and window, and Riley got Daddy's shotgun down off the wall. He loaded it with shaky hands and clicked it back. He stood in the middle of the floor waiting for that thing to bust the door down. We heard scratching on the door and heard it sniff like a big dog. We could hear it go from one end of the porch to the other. I could hear its toenails click on the wooden porch. It finally left the front porch, and then went around back, and it scratched its back on the big Chestnut out back.

"My brother Riley asked, 'What is that thing? Do you think it is some strange bear?'

We all just looked at each other because we all saw that thing walking around the side porch. It sniffed all around the windows, and then the sounds stopped. Riley cracked open the shutter on the back window and saw it go into the barn. The hounds were going crazy in their pens, and they were slobberin' and trying to dig out of that thing. Riley slowly closed the door, and then went into the kitchen and opened the door ever so slowly. Just then there was the biggest commotion coming out of that barn, and the chickens were flying around everywhere, and they were squawking, and old Jack, the mule, ran out kicking and bellowing, and running for his life. My older brother Elbert shot into the air over the barn, and that black critter came running out of the barn carrying about six chickens, and it was covered with feathers and dirt. It ran into the woods behind the barn. I remember being so scared that me and that pup were hunkered down in the corner of the bedroom. When Daddy got back, we all told him what had happened, and he went into the barn. That furry critter had killed about ten chickens and had scattered stuff all over the inside of the barn, and left a terrible odor all over the place. Daddy looked at its footprints in the mud. The footprints were like a man's, but when my Daddy put his size ten's in the critter's footprint, he could put both his feet, heel to toe, inside the whole footprint. Elbert showed Daddy the pieces of fur that was left where he scratched his back on the big tree just off from the house. The hair was too long for a black bear. A man came up that day on horseback with a long gun. He told Daddy that other farms in the area had livestock killed that night. They got a group of men with horses and dogs to go hunt the thing. They figured anything that big had to leave a big trail of broken twigs and stomped down grass, but the only tracks it made was when it had to step in mud. The excited dogs followed a scent trail for about fifteen miles, and then everyone gave up and came on back the next day. Daddy said there weren't any returning tracks, the animal or whatever it was, headed in one direction and that was north, and he was going steady fast."

Ida Mae stood up and walked over to the end of the porch and pointed down, and told us that right there on the steps you could see the claw marks. We all went over there and we could plainly see, right there on the rail by the steps were deeply cut claw marks into the wood. There were some other scratches on the porch wood close to the door and some on the steps. The claw marks were huge and deep, and I thought if that was the claw marks of a bear, it had to be humongous. We bumped heads trying to get a better look as we all just looked at each other with wild-eyed amazement.

Again she made us jump when she looked up at us and said, "I still can remember the smell of the rotten thing. Its scent lingered even after a couple of heavy rains. You know it was a musky smell, sort of like a skunk, or a muskrat."

Someone had mentioned Halloween after the scary stories, and the chatter started about things going on and a costume dance at their college, and a Halloween movie or something silly like that. Ida Mae's eyes and ears perked up when she heard this. She turned to the girl talking about Halloween parties and just started all over again.

"Up here we didn't have time for a lot of foolishness. You see honey, we didn't have to make up stories to scare little children by the firelight, all we had to do was listen to our elders or experience it for ourselves, and the stories were passed down and told, just as I am doing with you right now. We had enough to scare the devil out of us every day of the week, all year long. I am sure if the mountains up here could talk, we would have a hundred stories that would make the hairs on the back of your neck stand straight up. You must remember, this is an old place, with old stories, old families, and nature's own stories that are older and stranger than all."

Chapter IX

The Hardest Years
Were Yet to Come

We took some time between stories to stretch and move about, and of course, Ida Mae needed time to shift her body around a little bit. She would take advantage of these timely spacers with the greatest of ease, and she would lightly sip her tea. She chit-chatted with us and asked us what we wanted to do and if we had sweethearts, and asked what our parents did, just the usual small talk to mix up the time we had. We got back to settling in and back to business. After resting some, she continued where she left off.

"I know I have been talking about the good life that I have had from then to now, but in the early years, it was do or die. You should know about the old days. Back in the old days when my grandparents were kids, they worked from the time their little feet hit the floor, 'til the time those little feet went back to bed at night. They were lucky to get a hug or even get noticed during a workday, although they knew they were loved. If anyone even thought of such a thing as Halloween, I am sure as religious as they were, it would have been quickly erased from the mind. We didn't have time for the Devil, and they had to make time for God. All the families up here knew about All Hollow's Eve, and they told about it, but the occasion came and went without notice. Their life standards and values came from Ireland and Scotland. They were superstitious and religious at the same time. They kept their Sabbath holy and had Sunday dinners; they had Bible readings in the evenings at the kitchen table with an oil lamp.

"Change was not easily accepted here. The family figured, if we ain't used it in the past, then there wasn't any room or great desire for it in the present or the future. It was just a common assumption that if it had worked for the last one hundred years, it could keep on working just the same. If it was good enough for 'old great grandpap,' then we are not any better, and it will be good enough for all of us. We learned to make due with what we had. No out-side influence was ever needed up here on this mountain top."

Ida Mae sat back and said, "I remember one time, I was just a small child, I heard my momma talk about a few educated men that came around other mountain communities looking for music lyrics and old songs and stories the families passed down, and looking for arts and crafts. Our family wouldn't have anything to do with them because they weren't sure what they wanted from them. All the asking and no giving back in return just didn't sit right with my daddy. We found out later that those educated, city men went back and made mountain people look like a bunch of inbred idiots. A lot of the people took those fellows in and let them stay with them because they thought they were being neighborly, and showing their Christian kindness to a stranger. They all found out the hard way.

"The stories of the 'mountain folk' were in books and newspapers that read we were 'quaint' and lived in another century, like something in a sideshow. Strangers with binoculars and cameras tried to come up here. My daddy ran every one of those freeloaders off of this mountain. You know, a lot of people from the outside world looked down on us and called us "hill-billies" and "hicks," and just plain stupid, we are a lot of things, but never that! I'll tell you one thing that you can take to the bank; we never stood in line for anything. We never took a hand out. We didn't need a thing from the outside world. We never got nervous waiting for a cab to take us somewhere where you couldn't park a car. We never had suicides up here, we never had "nervous breakdowns" up here, and none of us ever got hit by a car or train, or had a problem with drugs. We left our doors unlocked because we just didn't have any thievery."

Ida Mae said after the outside world got interested in mountain folk, it was never the same up here. It seemed the other people down in the valley and upon other ridges not only lost faith in the mountain ways, but they lost their innocence after all the attention those city fellers stirred up making the 'hillbilly' curse. She told us that her daddy and some of his brothers, along with some of the women, turned the situation around. They were excellent woodworkers, and accustomed to making furniture and carving little farm animals. The women were seamstresses, and they made silly aprons, corn cob pipes, and corn shuck dolls. So, they carried down about one hundred and fifty pieces or so, down to the vegetable market on the river, and sold it all to those curious flatlanders, and made enough for flour, grain, and seed for the next year. We still sell items down there. It seems we all had the last laugh."

All Hail, The New King!

She looked us over carefully. We were listening closely and taking in every story, enjoying every minute, but we could tell the mood was starting to change. We all got quiet as before, only we became more involved with her conversation, and we knew those innocent days were long gone. It started to hit a little close to home, I guess. She knew it too.

"Talk of coal spread like wildfire. Everyone on the mountains and ridges was touched in one way or another. The coal companies had bought a lot of land and started mines around the area. There were small little mines scattered all around the county, and the big coal companies bought most of them out. Now that there were a lot of men working in the mines, the coal companies started to worry about the rumblings of men wanting a union. They knew this would limit their power over the workers and the amount of coal being hauled out. The big coal and steel companies and their investors, stood to lose a lot of money, and because they backed certain politicians, the government had to step in because the money and the power was up for grabs.

"The government said that those union leaders were communists and didn't believe in Jesus. They said everything they could to keep our boys in the mines working for only a couple of dollars for ten to fifteen hours a day.

The thieving politicians, along with the coal company stripped the people of their minerals, their land, their houses, their pride, their health, and their young men. No one outside of these mountains hardly ever knew that such things happened up here. There were murders and businesses burned, and things got pretty rough in the mountains. It seemed the outside world wanted to hear how ignorant the mountain people were, but they never heard of what our own government kept quiet. Have you young people ever heard of The Battle of Blair Mountain? The miners came from all over to support those miners who wanted a union. Both sides met with gunfire flying between them. The government sent airplanes there to drop bombs on our miners. I know it is the truth, I saw the planes fly over. Men were killed for trying to work and make honest wages for their families. It was a terrible time. I am sure you won't read it in your American History books at your school."

A guy from Marshall said. "We wouldn't bomb our own citizens in our own country over trying to establish a union."

"I just can't believe this would happen," said a student behind me.

"You go down to McDowell County Court House and everything I that I have told you, and more, is there on the public records for you to look up. If you history students want to read something really juicy, you can go to the Welch library and the Bluefield Library, and they have the newspapers telling all about it. There was a sheriff that was killed on the courthouse steps there by some hitmen that were hired by the coal company, because Sid Hatfield, the sheriff, tried to stop a blood bath in Matewan. Go look it up for your self, and when you read the facts about Matewan and The Battle of Blair Mountain, you tell folks what happened, ya hear?"

We all said, "Yes ma'am we will."

We were shocked. Why did this happen in America? *The Civil War was embarrassing enough, or so I thought.*

I was aware of the hard times going on right at that moment with the mines shutting down operations in many places, and people leaving the state to try and make a living. Some of the little community schools were closing and consolidating into larger schools. I was aware of the condition on the roads because of the coal trucks and how they got away with breaking every law there was on the highways. I guess 'King Coal' did have free reign over everything, even now.

Ida Mae spoke up and said, "The only way we escaped, I honestly believe that God was watching out over the families because they had respect for the land and didn't trust any outsiders to come up here. Our mountain is the tallest mountain around, but harder to navigate, and maybe that's why it is forgotten or just not worth the bother. Perhaps it was because this here is a wet mountain with caves. I don't know, but that in itself is a glorious blessing from God," she said so solemnly. We all were quiet, silently fighting off the tears.

She didn't look at us, as she kept her head down looking at her hands. It was apparent that she was in a thinking mode.

She continued, "...after the mine wars, nothing was the same up in the mountains all around us. Thank God, they didn't give up none of the close kin to that, but families lost close friends."

Mountain Momma...

"Our families were so sheltered and protected up here. They never had to put up fences in the beginning, but later in the early 1880's, people started wandering up and hunting and just nosin' around. So, for us to keep what was rightfully ours, and to keep people from killing our game and livestock, we had to fence. The livestock ran free for hundreds of years, and they never worried about where they were or what damage they did to someone's fields. Now, it is a different story. Some of the back fields were edged off with thicket so deep and dense, a rabbit couldn't get through it without being greased. So, they didn't fence those edges, and Daddy knew every landmark, so there wouldn't be any questions about land ownership. He knew each of our cows' and pigs' ears were notched, and the chickens never really wandered off. They did keep the horses, and mules, and those pesky goats fenced. Everybody up here knew what belonged to who. If something got out and was someplace it didn't need to be, including children, they were brought home by the finders. We all had a common interest; keeping a good life here on the mountain. Thank God that our ancestors claimed the land when the maps were drawn by the law, and paid their taxes.

"We all helped to mend our dirt roads after the winter freeze or bad summer storms. We all helped each other and still do to this day. If a storm or lightning, or a fire or mudslide destroys one of our houses up here, or a barn, we don't wait for some government agency to come and fix it. We take care of our own business in a timely fashion. If something was broken or a job needed to be done, we just did it. We clear out fallen trees, fix our roads, and fix things that need fixing. No questions asked. Our old people are taken care of, and our widows and widowers are loved and cherished, treated with respect, and everyone makes sure they have wood chopped, food on the table, a good dog for comfort, or a good house cat to keep the mice away. The older ones are seen and checked by a family member every day if they have not moved in with family. Not one of us was ever found dead, alone in our bed days later. We never die alone up here. We all are family. We know everybody and call them by their first names, and we know their children, and if one of us see's someone else's child acting up, we call them down and tell on them. Then the parents take care of that child, and no one gets mad or bent out of shape for butting into the family business. We watch out for each other. Seems that if the country would go back to such simpler ways things would just be better off.

"All of us feel if a child asks a question, and if he is old enough to ask and understand, he is answered the best way we know how. We never did talk baby talk or use 'silly nonsensical' words after the child is six or so months old. Our babies learned to talk early and walk early. Everyone takes the time to teach our children early how to survive up here. Our children can go it alone in the woods for weeks and live off the land by the time they are ten years old. By that age, our girl children know how to cook almost as well as their mothers. Our girls can peel potatoes and apples at least at six years old, and never cut themselves. Can you see a spoiled, little city girl peel an apple at that age? Our boys can do a day's work alongside their fathers and can build and mend just as good as the older men. We make sure of that. Our boys can hunt and fish by the age of six. We take care of their future, whatever that may be."

One of the girls from Beckley asked, "Why do you teach your young people all this stuff at an early age? Don't they miss their childhood? What about sex education?"

We all turned to look at Ida Mae to see what reaction would show in her eyes and her voice. She got a serious look in her eyes that looked like she was worried.

She answered, "Our children learn to read and write early and to reason and cypher. After all, we all read and write almost every day. The learning never stops. One never knows what may befall us. We just know to be prepared for anything and everything at any time. There were lanterns nailed to a couple of trees out from the house a'ways, just in case you were out there and needed light, maybe to help with finding the pigs or the cows. I bet the President of the United States could not have been safer from intruders than we were. I bet he wouldn't last a couple of days in our woods. Our five-year-old children know what is dangerous and what is allowed, they know to follow strict rules early.

"Fun was never hard to find on the mountain, we had plenty of it, but everything has a time, and everything has a reason up here. Just like Ecclesiastes, everything has a season. A time to work and a time to play, a time to wake and a time to sleep, a time to have babies and a time to wait for that blessing. Our children don't lack for a thing. Nothing was ever kept from our children. We lived on a farm with farm animals everywhere. The mating of the animals on the farm or in the woods is natural, and there were no questions that we would not answer as best we could. Sometimes they would ask questions in detail, and according to the child, the mom or dad would tackle that subject. We always considered sex as a beautiful thing and a sacred thing between a married man and a woman. After all, we are just animals too, and it is nature's way of keeping the species going. Children up here are taught that it is something we don't make fun of, it is not dirty or lusted after when grown. That's why we get married, so we don't make fools of ourselves. The young people know what is right and what is wrong. Yes, mistakes have happened up here, but it is not anyone's fault. I have helped bring many of the cutest little mistakes into this world. Understand this, mistakes are made by married people just as easily as unmarried people. We are human, and God knows what we are capable of, doesn't he? We live by the Bible and all of God's commandments as best we can. Our young people know what is what. Children are raised God-fearing, and they continue as they grow up, to live as God's children up here."

She went on to tell us that as far as fun goes, it was not all work and no play up here. They all had games they played after their chores. They make sure that the children have a well-balanced life. They are not left to be tended by others, they don't have babysitters, and the children never play too far from the house, but they have a great time being raised here on the mountain. Besides, fun isn't just for children. They all enjoy themselves when they can, but they take their chores seriously and first things first. They go camping up on the other ridge, or down by the river where they fish for a couple of days. They go on picnics all through the summer and have hayrides in the fall. She also reminded us of how much fun they had during apple and berry picking time. Winter came with an awakening of more fun ahead, as they loved sledding in the deep snow and being pulled by one of the workhorses. Even today, they build snow forts and have snowball fights alongside a big bonfire. In the summertime, they all knew of a waterfall and pool just down from the barn, and they would head out there no matter how old or young. The young people swing on grape vines and fall into the water. They will splash around all afternoon, until almost suppertime. In the evenings when the sun goes down, many times the family sits on the front porch right here, and all the kin who like to pick some music, even now, they come and play until they are all just too tired to play and sing any more."

She thought for a second about what she was about to say.

"I pray all of us up here have wonderful memories that will last as long as mine, and the memories will be handed down as all our ancestors' memories have. We all still journal today. I have written in my journals since I was around ten years old. My journals are not with this bunch. They will stay in my bedroom. We continue the writing tradition that came with the clans on that boat ride across the Atlantic. Our families have stories to tell. We don't want to change."

She looked like she wanted to say more. I couldn't read her face, but I could feel she wanted to open up and release it all. She twisted her lace handkerchief in her hands, as she struggled with this story. She spoke with a saddened tone of voice

"I have to talk about this. In other parts of the Appalachian mountain range, a new way of life and thinking was uncovered. Now, no matter how hard one tries to protect their mountain way of life, sometimes bad things creep into our lives. I like to compare these things as a mother with her children. The 'Momma' is the mountain way of life. The 'Children,' naturally, are the mountain people. A mother tries to protect her babies the best way she can, but trying to protect a large number of children makes it hard to do such an enormous task. Those big city coal operators and those big city gas people wanted us to change to their ways of thinking. They desired to get rich off what has been under our feet for four hundred years."

Ida Mae reached for the box of tissues on the table beside her and blew her nose, and wiped her eyes. We were uncomfortable watching this sweet little lady tear up. We looked at each other and wondered what she was going to tell. We were ready and primed. With eager fingers on the record buttons, we waited. She finally pulled herself together and spoke with a little crack in her voice.

"After they pulled a lot of our young men into the dark mines, the big companies made them think of bigger and better ways, and telling them they don't need nothing else but the mines. Then the companies started shutting down, leaving the men without a job, and for the first time, they found out what owing for something is and not being able to pay for it, nor did they have anything to do. Some of 'Mountain Momma's' babies strayed. Many new problems grew in the mountains that had never grown here before. The mines would take them at thirteen years old or even younger. They didn't get educated because they didn't need to finish school if the they worked in the mines. While working in the mines, the men made more money there than the teachers, farmers, or traders ever thought about making. Then when the mines shut down, welfare took the place of our pride. This mountain pride was being swallowed up by big city politics, and every evil finger was in the pie, taking what wasn't theirs in the first place. It made a whole new list of sins. Some of 'Momma's' children began cheating the government, which was the newest way to make money, and not sweating doing any real work. Lying became easy, and greed grew up here real fast.

The government moved people in this area to help the mountain people lie, cheat, and steal so that they could get an easy payday. Once they became influenced by the 'modern new ways,' and how to get into debt making house payments and land payments and taxes, the bosses told them that this was the new "American Way" of doing things. Now, don't get me wrong, the lure of quick money did have an attraction. My daddy and three of my brothers left the farm to work evening shifts in the mines so we could have things from the store. We bought hard to come by things, but they never went into debt at the company stores. Daddy knew the snares there, and taught his boys well in that area. Some came back to 'Momma Mountain's' loving arms and picked up where they left off, and was glad in the final choice they made. Our menfolk didn't all go in the mines, and those that did go it was only temporary work. God, family, and farm were priorities."

Angie Mayberry, a dark-haired beauty from War who was attending Marshall College, asked quickly, "What about your family? How did this change affect the family?

Ida quickly answered that question. "My family, thank God, did not put all their eggs in one basket. Oh, we got hurt alright, we lost some of our dear people and dearest friends to the cities, but most of our kinfolk got out before the mines took their souls. We could not give the time that they wanted. We were just too busy trying to keep the fields planted and cut, and living. Like I said, even my daddy worked in the mines, and some of our boys did too, so they had to juggle a couple of jobs to make ends meet. Some of our menfolk kept the farms going, and worked in the mines in the evening and during the times when the crops didn't need tending. They didn't work in the mines during harvest and planting time. Even though the mines took my daddy, I guess God did watch out for my kin. We helped the other families that could not juggle farms and mines. I think more than not, the young men saw that the money that the mines paid was like giving wine to a drunkard. It was a dangerous drink. The company store made it so easy to trade with them and pay with company money called script. Lord have mercy, they thought they were rich. Many of our friends from down in the valley wanted to leave and go to big cities that promised a better life. A lot went to Detroit, Cleveland, Charlotte, and towns in many other directions. It was a dark time for 'Momma's' children. Northerners were trying to buy up every piece of land in the valleys for the railroads and highways, and trying to buy mineral rights from anyone who owned a land deed. They wanted the mountains too, but they didn't get very much from our neck of the woods. 'Momma's' children that she held closer kept the family together. Our families still held over 15,000 acres of rolling hills, and good pasture land. Of course now a'days, a few mountain tops over, you can see on a clear day how they have taken off the tops of the mountains for strip mining. They are like thieves in the night."

Ida Mae cleared her throat and began again...

"One time I remember as if it were yesterday, I was about eight years old at the time, some people finally found their way up Slip Creek, and said we owed taxes. Like I said about Daddy, he was one to turn a dollar faster than anyone could. It seems Daddy knew some real secrets about the county court people, including the taxman, and a few of those politicians owed my daddy money from gambling deals down at the river house, and he had made an arrangement that was agreeable by all. Those government men paid the taxes and seemed they were paid off for about twenty-five years after that. But, soon after that, those old company boys tried to do something about our land rights and mineral rights, and the company found three bodies lying on the county courthouse's doorstep one early Monday morning. The doctor told them that they had drowned. Those three bodies lying on that wooden porch were three and a half miles away from any deep water. I think they got the message. Like back in the old days, the voice of our ancestors told the family to protect what was ours. No one ever admitted to the crime, and no one was ever charged in the mysterious deaths.

"The coal company decided that they would leave our 'legal rights' alone. But they were constantly trying to get to us one way or another. We had a cave on our land, located down near the base of our mountain. One day a few men went in and decided to mine it for the company without asking. We watched as they brought their wagons and picks and shovels, and their northern workers to claim their prize. Late one evening as some of the men went down to see what was going on, they planted some explosive gifts inside that little operation. The next day, we watched as the explosion blew wagons, picks, shovels, men, and mules all the way to the river. They gave up on my family and our land. Money was not to be made off of us."

She stopped and smiled with a different little twinkle in her eye as she told us, "We still have that little market down the road. Those big-shot mine operators stop all the time to get snacks, a bottle of coke, or buy gifts. They would buy our produce, seed, and moonshine. Did I say moonshine?" Ida Mae laughed out loud, and said in a giggly voice, "That is another story altogether."

She stood and stretched a little bit and said, "I have to go into the house for a minute, you young people don't stray too far, and I'll be back to chat with you all in just a minute."

We understood it to be a bathroom break. We all had to stand up and stretch too. Man, I was getting sore sitting and writing as young as I was, I can imagine how Ida Mae felt sitting in that old rocker looking down and around at us. How much time had passed was not the question, and I didn't even think of looking at my watch. The only question I had in mind was what I was going to ask her next. I can only assume that everyone else's wheels were turning as fast as mine. *What a movie this would make I thought to myself. A wonderful play! Oh, my God! I could get rich writing about this in a novel! She would have to play the lead. Who else could tell it like herself, and who else had those intense blue eyes and that little cackle that was so mischievous? How could you train an actor to be that authentic and believable?* I had to go to the bathroom too, so I just peed behind the house up the hill a little way, behind a big oak. My mind was still whirling around even as I stood. *What in the world was I thinking? Dr. Summers would laugh his ass off at me right now, wouldn't he? My mind is running away with me.* I zipped up and quickly walked back to the water pump, got a drink and washed my hands, and came back around to the cabin.

What was that delicious aroma? Man, somebody was cooking something that smelled like nothing I had ever smelled before. Okay, I had to get a hold of my thoughts. I had to find my seat and get ready for the next story she was going to tell. She came out with a tray full of ham biscuits, still hot from the oven. I believe to my soul that was the best thing that I had ever eaten. Everyone grabbed one, and I had another refill of that iced tea. Ida Mae Cook sat back down in her rocker, got her cushion just right, and brushed those bothersome white hairs around her forehead away from her face. I grabbed another biscuit.

********Chapter X********
Wallace Avery
Was My First Love

The next question came from a very attractive co-ed that sat the closest to me.

The girl was blond and flirty, and I had my eye on her all day. She was from Duke University, and you could tell she had money by the way she was dressed and acted, and of course, by the Mustang she was driving. Anyway, she quickly asked the question we all wanted to ask.

"Ida Mae, did you ever get to date or court anybody from up on the mountain, and what was your love life like?"

Ida Mae's eyes had a little twinkle in them, and a sneaky little grin pressed the wrinkles around her mouth into a smooth, up-turned, crescent moon shape.

"I was not an ugly girl, so I had a few boys that wanted to catch my attention. Lordy, they acted like pure fools. I was impressed by a few of them, but they were just fleeting moments. We all, at the time, had seasonal work to do. While at church and school, I had noticed a couple of real lookers, but I just wasn't that interested during that time in my life. Guess I was just too busy with the horses and the other animals around the place. We all were hard workers up here, so there wasn't much idle time for courting until the courting bug bit me, and then I made sure I had the time. It was hard to fall for any of the boys when my brothers and cousins dared anyone to touch me. When the mountain girls court everyone watches out for them." She laughed as she told us the rest of the story.

She plainly said, "My love life is a simple tale. I have been in deep love twice in my whole life, and that's enough for any female. Now, mind you, I have been 'in like' and infatuations before a couple of times down the road, but none of those silly things ever amounted to anything special."

Ida Mae smiled as she was thinking back to those days. She said that in her younger days she would have never talked out loud about her love life or her private life to anyone, but now that she has grown older, she just didn't give a hoot.

She said that she had to set the situation, like a play, so we all would understand how this all came to be. She wanted to explain how and why the coal company had a lot to do with her first love story. It all started with the growth of the new coal company. She said that they brought down engineers and geologists from up north to assist in the planning and running of the mining part of the business. The mapping of the tunnels and taking of ore samples were all new ways of doing things at that time. It became scientific, and they needed men that had been specially educated for that purpose.

There in the bottom land, the coal company built a large community building where they had about five small apartments or living spaces upstairs, and there were offices and meeting rooms, and a large room for dances or entertainment. They would put up some of their big shots or business executives. Why they called that big building the Community Building, no one will never know. Only the main bosses and the superintendent's family could use the great ballroom for parties and banquets. The coal mining community never set foot in that part of the building, unless they were cooks, waiters, or janitors. She said they would have elaborate parties, where everyone would dress up in the fanciest dress and eat the fanciest foods while they listened to orchestras bussed in from up north. As it seems, they couldn't curse it too much because it made a lot of jobs for some of the people who needed jobs. There was a great need for cooks and maids. She said the pay wasn't that good, but it sure did help, especially the widows that were young enough to work hard and long. Other women got jobs cleaning the boss's houses as well. Laundry became a good business with those who could wash and iron. If those mine people needed anything done, there were always folks who could do the job.

When the big shots from up north would come down to attend one of the balls, they would always have a company picnic on that Sunday that followed. The summer picnics were the only time the workers and their families would be allowed to mingle with the big shots. It was on one of these summer picnics held by the company, that changed Ida Mae Meade's life.

There were a lot of people there that she didn't know of course, but some of the young people running around she knew because of school. All the families went to the picnic, mostly because it was free food. The company thought that if they gave the poor workers one day of food, fun, and games, that everyone would be happy, satisfied, and loyal for the rest of the year.

The whole family was excited about the picnic that summer, and they could not wait for the time to come. She remembered it to the day, as she said it was on the Fourth of July. The excitement of the picnic could only be compared with the wonderment of the fireworks that had been shipped there from New York.

Ida Mae's parents, Jake and Rosebud, sat with some other miners that Jake knew. They found a picnic table under the willows next to the creek, and enjoyed the shade and the breeze. Ida Mae said that her momma and daddy were a little uncomfortable being there, knowing how her daddy felt about mining, but they eventually loosened up and enjoyed themselves.

There were long tables covered with white tablecloths, and there were servers and busy people working to make sure everyone got in the right line. The tables were placed on a perfectly flat spot on the flat grassy area, down close to the river. She said that there were folding chairs and tables setting everywhere. Ida Mae said her daddy had many friends there, as most of them were his moonshine customers. They all came up to her daddy to shake his hand. Most of the women there knew her momma, as they all went to the same church. So they all had something to talk about and to keep them from being bored.

There were special events that involved everyone who wanted some fun. Some of the men threw horseshoes and prizes were given for the best thrower, and there were sack races all day along, a hammer throwing contest for the men, and a skillet throwing contest which was just for the womenfolk. There was also a cake auction and a pie auction that was a highlight of the afternoon, as well as the watermelon eating contest. She said her brothers won the watermelon eating contest. We all had a good laugh over that comment.

The company had big brick cookers built, and they roasted a whole beef and a large pig, along with tons of potatoes and ears of corn. They had other people come in with a wagon full of beer barrels. Another wagon was behind the beer wagon, and it had the desserts and watermelons. She said she quickly got bored, so she walked through the willow bushes and down to the creek. She found a place where the water was shallow, and the big rocks that were there were just perfect to jump from one to the other. She said that since she was somewhat athletic, she could have jumped clean across the creek to the other side if she had a notion. She found a big rock to sit on, and her momma would have killed her if she had known that Ida Mae had taken off her stockings and her shoes and put her feet in the water.

Oh, my heart...

This is when she crossed her legs and set up straight, and said, "I was sitting on that big flat rock on the edge of the creek just letting the cool, clear water run over my feet, when a man's voice said, 'A crawdad will get your toes!' I jumped as his voice broke the silence, and almost fell in the water. As I turned around, there stood the best-looking boy I had ever seen in my life. I wasn't that interested in boys at that time, you know, but when I saw him, I quickly changed my mind. He had a cap on his head, and he wore white and blue pinstriped shirt with rolled up sleeves and dark blue pants with suspenders. His clothes were not patched and looked new. His shoes looked new because they did not have a bit of scuff or coal marks on them. By the look of him, I knew that he wasn't from around these parts. After I caught my breath, I just bluntly asked, 'Well, who are you?'

"He said, 'My name is Wally, and I work down at the mine, I live at the company boarding house down beside the company store.' He was a bold one. I told him that I wasn't supposed to talk to strangers and I turned my back on him and went to another rock, so I could put my stockings and shoes back on. After all, it was not appropriate for him to see my naked feet. He followed me over to the other rock and sat down beside of me. I was in shock. He just started talking to me about the weather and crawdads, and fish and snakes as I looked at him in amazement. I was trying to have a private moment with my stockings and shoes. I told him to turn his head as I put my stuff on. He did but kept on talking. I never had in my life heard a man talk so much.

"He did have a strange accent, and it made me want to listen to the beautiful words coming out of his mouth that was like music. We must have talked for about three hours and found out everything there was to know about each other. Wally was a young engineer that the coal company brought down in these parts from Pittsburgh, Pennsylvania. He was staying at the company house until they could find him suitable quarters while he was here. I was almost fifteen, and he was twenty-one, just turned. He said that I looked older than fifteen, which pleased me of course. He asked me where I went to church, and I told him in the summer we would go down to the church at the end of the hollow. He knew exactly where it was, and he told me that he was going to start attending there from now on and we could talk for a while after church. I informed him that the older people always stayed and talked to catch up on the farming and mining gossip, and with each other after service. They usually remained about an hour or so."

A most rememberable summer...

"Momma and Daddy couldn't believe how religious I got that summer, wanting' to go to church every Sunday and Wednesday night. The whole summer Wally and I talked every Sunday and Wednesday night. We also went to the church suppers they had the first Friday night of every month. I think it was in early September, he asked me if I wanted to go for a walk while the families all talked. We walked a slow pace down the dirt road past the church. He took my hand in his and I thought my heart would beat clean out of my chest. Lordy, I was smitten. We smiled at each other and kept on walking. When I told him it was time to turn around and head on back the long road to the church, he turned my head with his gentle hand and held my chin. I was frozen at the gaze of his sky-blue eyes. He leaned into me ever so slowly and kissed me right on the lips. My first real kiss and it was a doozy! I thought I would fly right up in the air at that very moment. I knew right then and there that religion had just paid off. Thank you, God! You know what, that was eighty-five years ago, and I remember that sweet kiss to this day. I am sure you girls remember your first kiss, right? A girl never forgets her first kiss. All my girl cousins had told me what my first kiss would be like, but my first kiss beat their exaggerations by a mile. Of course, I was kissing a man instead of one of those silly boys. Guess that made a big difference. We walked back and didn't say a word to each other. I think we were just caught up in the moment and didn't need words, but from then on until the end of summer, I got kissed every Sunday, Wednesday, and at the church suppers. He wrote me letters during the cold part of the winter and sometimes I got to see him when I went into town with daddy or with one of my brothers.

"Wally became friends with my brothers and knew my daddy because they all worked together at sometimes at the mines. He finally approached my daddy on my seventeenth birthday and told him that he admired me and wanted to come calling, if that would be allowable. Daddy said he would have to talk it over with Momma. So, Daddy invited him up to dinner that Saturday night, so they could talk it over.

"I had never been so excited about anything in my life. We didn't get much company at the house, living way up on top of a steep hollow the way we did, so it was a special occasion just to have an outsider to come to the cabin, not to mention how important it was for me.

Momma pan-fried three fresh killed chickens, made a huge pan of biscuits with chicken gravy, and had fried potatoes, buttered garden peas, and corn. She sliced up a big onion and opened up a jar of stewed apples.

"Momma took pride in her 'put up apples.' Because we had such a large orchard, we had many jars of apples in one form or another. Momma was a master of anything that had to do with cooking and preserving anyway. She could make a pie or cobbler that would melt in your mouth. Lordy, my momma had a way with pie crusts, and she taught all her daughters and nieces, and granddaughters how to do it, but no one could duplicate it, not even me, and I watched her every time. She was just one of those gifted cooks."

Ida Mae continued...

"I remember she sat out a fresh cold pitcher of buttermilk and a bowl of sweet made butter. My daddy used to call butter 'cow salve.' I loved hearing him call butter that, and all the children would just laugh out loud when he said it. I think of him every time I see freshly made butter.

"When Wally arrived, he was out of breath and sat on the porch while all the kids swarmed around him. I think he was a little awestruck at all the children our family had. Even Daddy's coon hounds came up on the porch to get a sniff of our new visitor. They were satisfied with his smell and jumped off the porch, then went back under it to get to their cool, dark place of relaxation.

"Supper wasn't quite ready yet, so I showed him around the barn and the animal stalls, the spring houses, the smokehouse, and the summer kitchen, and of course I showed him the outdoor toilet. He was really shocked by all the things we had up here. Finally, we washed up and we went into the house and sat at our long table in the kitchen. Daddy said the blessing, and Momma started passing the bowls of food. Wally was a real eater. He just made himself at home and ate like the other boys. It was a good thing Momma knew about how much young men eat, guess she learned that from her own boys and her brothers. She used her own multiplication system and came out with the correct amount of food every time.

"Wally pushed back his chair and put both hands on his stomach and sighed, 'Mrs. Cook, I have been witness to some of the finest cooks in Pennsylvania and other places, and I do believe that none of those fancy cooks could out cook you on any given day.' Wally defiantly said all the right things that day. My momma lived with that compliment 'til the day that she died. He complimented my daddy too. Wally told my daddy how accomplished and resourceful he was with everything he did on this mountain, and thought Daddy was a genius. Wally said that when he viewed the sawmill and the way the farm and dairy were operated, he was inspired. He told Daddy that he just couldn't see how he did all those things and still worked in the mines. Wally also told Daddy that he was a shining example of what being a real man should be. My daddy was pretty proud that day too. If Wally had wanted to whisk me away with him to Timbuktu that very evenin', it would have been just fine with Daddy and Momma. Wally knew it too. He asked Daddy if we could go walking down the road together, and Daddy told Wally it would be fine.

"We walked and openly held hands. The hounds decided to go as our escorts up the road. We walked up the hill to the back of the large meadow, and I showed Wally our family cemetery. I opened the rusty iron gate, and we walked inside. I told him who everyone was and told him that we had written journals from everyone up here. All those graves were my kin, and we honored them all the time. He looked at the gravestones and read each name and asked questions about them.

"He told me that one day we both would lay here together side by side. I looked at him and said that people outside the family were not allowed to be buried here. I was a little slow. He told me he would be family before long if I would agree to marry him in the spring. I jumped up and put my arms around his neck, and he swung me around as I said loudly, 'Yes Wallace Avery, I will marry you!' He stopped swinging me around and still held me tight with my feet off the ground, and he kissed me long and hard that time, and it almost took the very breath from my lungs. This kiss was different, and it almost scared me. I trembled and he held me even closer. I didn't know that he was that strong of a man. He told me that he had loved me from the first time he saw me wading in the creek at the picnic. He never put me down, and he kissed me again in the same manner. Finally, one of daddy's hounds bellered out and scared the wits out of us both. The timing of the interruption, you could say, was in the nick of time. We were rattled back into our senses and I looked around at all the graves of my people, and felt ashamed of my actions, yet, I wanted them to see the man I was going to marry and spend eternity with. He couldn't have picked a more special spot to ask me to marry him. We were standing on sacred ground.

"We walked back to the house just a little faster than when we left, and we sat on the porch. Momma gave us another piece of apple pie with a cup of fresh coffee. After we finished the pie, Wally asked my daddy if just the two of them could take a walk over to the barn and talk privately. Momma was standin' in the door and looked over at me and grinned, and I looked embarrassed and gave her a sheepish grin. About thirty minutes later Daddy and Wally came back across the yard, and Daddy yelled out loud, 'There's going to be a fine weddin' here in the spring!'

"I jumped up from the swing and put my arms around my daddy's neck and thanked him with a big kiss on the cheek. Momma and Daddy went into the kitchen and left us outside.

I asked him what did Daddy say, and he said that Daddy told him, 'Boy, I believe you are a good man, but if you lay a hard hand on her or hurt her in any way, you'll be a good dead man.'

Wally's eyes were large, and he was still nervous, and he told me that he would always love me and put me on a pedestal. He said, 'I won't ever be cruel to you or hurt your feelings, or be unfaithful to you, so help me God.' Bless his sweet heart, he was so serious with big 'ol tears in his eyes.

"Daddy told Wally that we could be married down in our little church or up here on the mountain. Wally said it didn't matter to him, whatever or where ever I picked. Wally told me it didn't matter to him since all his family was dead and he didn't have any close family except us. He said we could talk about it the next day, as he had to be getting on down the road because it was getting pretty dark and he had to go to work the next morning. I told him I wanted it announced at church the next Sunday, and he agreed.

"I watched him walk out down the road as his head went down, down, and finally out of sight over the hill. The sun was settin' the most magnificent orange and purple colors. With this display in the sky, I took it as a good sign from God. I went in to help Momma clean up the kitchen and wash the dishes. We didn't talk, except that she thought he would make a fine, upstanding husband. Daddy came into the kitchen and sat at the table, and said that when the time came and we had a few days dry weather, we could have a cabin built in a couple of weeks with the help of his brothers and the kids. He said that the cabin could be built right next to Momma and Daddy's cabin. I told Daddy that I would love living next to him, and I was sure that Wally would love it too. I was so excited about the idea of having my own cabin and being a wife.

"When I went to bed, I tried to sleep, but thoughts of curtains and furniture along with dishes and quilts flew around in my head. I lay there for hours thinking about the kiss, the wedding, sleeping with Wally in the same bed, and the gifts and the party afterward. Visions of feather ticks for our bed, and pillows, and thinking of a good life finally gave way to a peaceful sleep.

"Sometime before the sun came up, I was awakened by the most dreaded of all sounds, the mine emergency whistle. There had been an accident at the mine. Everyone in the house threw off the covers and got dressed immediately. Daddy was out the door before I even got my shoes on. Two of my brothers, Riley and Daniel, had worked the graveyard shift and they were in the mine with most of my friends and a few of my cousins. Daddy rode the fastest horse down the road, my two older sisters and a brother rode the mule behind him, and I told Momma to stay and not to worry, we would make sure everything was all right. She stood at the door pale and wringing her hands. Even the little ones were up and knew the seriousness of the moment. They knew to be quiet and not to ask Momma any questions.

"I took off by foot and went through the through the woods that I knew like the back of my hand. I was as fleet as a doe and was sure-footed. I got there just minutes after daddy did. People were already standing all around the office and outside of the fence when I got there. I saw Wally and called to him. He came over and opened the gate so Daddy and me could get inside of the fenced area. He told us that the top in one section had fallen in, and he didn't know much of anything else until someone came out of that mine. There was a lot of rubble inside, so they had to work hard so they could bring those boys out. Some of the miners that had escaped the main fall were out sitting and being attended by other miners and office workers. Only a few minutes had passed by the time I had arrived there, and I was still out of breath when kinfolk of the miners, friends, and preachers began to gather at the gate. All wanting answers and praying together.

"I knew the routine, I had seen it many times before. We just had to sit and wait until someone came with news. I remember seeing those pitiful families before, crying because they had the sad news that one of their loved ones had been killed or badly injured. Now, it was the Meades, the Cooks, and the Jewells who were waiting there. Doctors from all the surrounding areas were coming in buggies and on horse back just to be of some help and comfort. All the business from up and down the river closed, and they came to the mine site. Women were making coffee and serving sandwiches to the people. Time seemed to drag and go in slow motion until we heard a voice saying, 'they're bringing' them out!'

"I stood as close as they would let me to see who was coming out of the mine. I heard the wagon before I saw it. The smoke and steam made it hard to see. The wagon was full of miners, and with the coal dirt on them, they all looked the same. My daddy ran to the wagon and pulled his two boys off that wagon, and they fell to the ground crying, and he hugged his boys with all that he had. My brothers had been saved from the dragon's mouth. That was the first time I had ever seen my father openly cry like a baby. Everybody was crying. This group of men that were brought out were the lucky ones. There were other men trapped on the back side of the roof fall. Riley and Daniel and my cousins were safe except I think, maybe one didn't make it. Riley said that he heard tapping and voices on the other side of the fall. They were alive. All the bosses that were on this side of the mine got their rescue gear and extra mules, horses, and ropes, along with the wagons to carry out the debris. I watched Wally run to the office and come out with maps and put them on a makeshift table. All the bosses came over, and they talked fast and worked feverishly. Some stayed to read the plans, but Wally ran back inside the office and came out with an armload of stuff, and I saw that he had extra lanterns and canteens. His assistant ran out of the office behind him, carrying' a large wooden box that was a first aid kit.

"Wally turned to me, ran back over, kissed me, and said that he was going to get those men out for their families. He told me to go on home with Daddy Jake and my brothers to tell Momma the good news, and not to wait for him, that he would be on up to the house as soon as he got them out and got cleaned up. I smiled at him in a way that he knew that I would not go home without him. He ran with the others into the gapin' black mouth of the steaming dragon.

Everyone cheered as they watched Wally and the rest of the men run to save their boys. I sat down on the grassy knoll just out of the way to wait for my Wally. Daddy came over and told me to get on home and help Momma with chores, and I told him I would be there as soon as Wally came out. They left and rode on up the mountain without me. I had to stay to know that my friends were alright. The sun had come up and was warming up the day. I curled up in the grass and tried to close my eyes as I waited alone. While lying on the ground, I felt a strange rumble and heard a strange hissing sound. I rose up, and everyone was quiet. Suddenly, I heard the biggest 'boom!,' and a metal wagon part landed within a foot of my head. There were dead mules, wagon parts, picks, and shovels laying all over the place. Smoke came bellering out of that hole, and we heard another explosion. Everyone was running, and it became a frenzy of people hollering and screaming. Stuff was still blowin' out of the mine, and I ran closer to the big oak just by the gate. I stood and watched in horror as one man came crawling out of the mouth of the mine and was badly burned. They said he was Wally's office assistant. He died about an hour later in a tent they had set up for the injured. They said that he was on his way out of the mine to get more men to help when the explosion happened.

"It took an hour for the dust to clear and the smoke to move off so we could see what was happening. The smoke would have been there longer if it had not started to rain. Miners from another mine came in wagons to help. I watched them come and go, shaking their heads. You could see a sunk in place on the side of the mountain. It looked like the whole mountain had fallen in on itself. I couldn't believe what I was seeing. I have no idea how many hours I sat there under that tree. I couldn't move. I just sank down to the ground and hugged that old oak while people were swirling around me in a strange dance of fear and sadness. I will always remember the sound of women screaming and crying. People were trying to go into the mine to pull the dirt, rocks, and twisted metal out. I sat there, I think all night long, sobbing. I remember my daddy finally riding up and lifting me up on his horse; he put me in the saddle, and he rode behind me, holding me all the way up the mountain. Momma bathed me and washed my hair, and put me to bed. I stayed in bed for a week. I didn't want to see anybody or be around a soul. Momma forced me eat some broth every day, but I couldn't eat anything else. I cried every waking minute. The family walked around the house like they had cotton balls on their feet. Then finally, on the seventh day, Momma came into the room, went to the windows and pulled up the sash, pulled back the curtains, and pulled the covers off me. I didn't know what got into her. Momma said, 'Enough is enough. Get yourself out of this bed and jump back into life, girl. The Bible says to mourn for a week, and your week is up!' She also told me that mountain people didn't have time to mourn for their dead. We didn't have that luxury. If I was woman enough to get married, then I was woman enough to carry a woman's burdens. I never took to my bed again in sorrow."

Ida Mae paused and thought for a short while, and then spoke again.

"The owner of the mines put up a bronze plaque on the entrance to the mine. It tells of the mine disaster, and the names of the men lost in the cave in, and the names of the heroes who tried to save them. The name of Wallace Avery is the first name on the list. They never retrieved the bodies of the men. They just closed that part of the mine forever. Since Wally didn't have any family, it was perfectly alright. He wanted to be buried on the mountain anyway. I brought flowers to the entrance for a couple of years after that. I still think of dear Wally every time I pass by the mine gate on my way to church. I never felt guilty for my feelings for Wally, even though I learned to love again in my life. I know Wally would have wanted me to be happy.

"Like my momma said, we mountain folk do not have the time to mourn or wither up and die until it is time, and when it is time, we will do it gracefully and with dignity, and without fear."

It was so quiet on that porch. All of us were wiping tears, and the sniffs probably scared off the birds that had just been singing. I took a deep breath and turned the page of my spiral notebook. I had just been taught about living and dying in the past few minutes. Having never experienced tragedy in my life, and I pray I never have to go through what she had to endure.

I understand that the story that I am going to write will be a "living story" instead of a "telling story." I cannot imagine the hardships, the pain, and grief she must have had to conquer to live. The main idea that came across to my mind is, live to the fullest capacity of your life. We have to make do with the hand dealt to us; we have to make it count.

Chapter XI

The Story About Little Sulie

A s Ida Mae promised, she would answer more questions as soon as she got settled back into her chair. She fluffed her cushions and sat back, stretched her arms out, put her wrinkled hands upon her legs, and gave that look that meant it was time to start again. The first student to speak at this moment was from Radford Women's College. She asked about the article in all the newspapers about a black woman, whom the Cook's had harbored and protected until she could make her way up north during the Civil War. This was the story that started the whole thing about Ida Mae and her connection to a black family up north. The black family was interviewed by *The Morning Show* and *Evening News*, and the whole world had become aware of Appalachia and this one hundred-year-old white woman whom kept secrets of historic value that the world wanted to know.

"Lordy, I don't know what all the hoopla is all about," she said as she turned to us.

"My grandmaw helped some poor little girl in need. That is the code up here in the mountains. We do not turn any of God's injured creatures away, man nor beast. Well, I just couldn't figure it out, why people wanted to know all about this," she said as she just shook her head."

I knew most of the story, because my editor filled me in. The family helped a run-a-way slave that made it to the mountains. The black woman's grandchildren and great grandchildren wanted to meet Ida Mae and the rest of her family to let them know how everything turned out, and to thank the family for saving their ancestor. Ida Mae had no idea or even considered that the story had reached *National News Press, Canadian News Service,* American television, everybody in West Virginia, and to every politician in the tri-state area. Ida Mae was just plain shocked that anyone else knew the story. She told us that she knew the story that had been passed down from woman to woman in the family, but she hadn't read the details for many years. She said that she had to go back into her journals to freshen up her memory, and when she finally found her grandmaw's journal, sure enough there it was, the story of a young African slave woman named Sulie. I watched her set back in her rocker and she looked up to the sky, then closed her eyes. It was obvious she was thinking about years passed, and she smiled as she started remembering the stories that her momma, her aunts, and her grandmaw had told her, and her sisters.

Still, with the misty look of memory in her eyes, she spoke. "Well, one of the boys was out hunting one morning, a few miles down in the valley. I think it was Uncle Elbert, he found Sulie, half dead, lying still on the creek bank. She had cuts and bruises all over her body, and her feet were bleeding, she was wet, shaking, and was unconscious. Uncle Elbert wrapped her in a blanket, put her on his horse, and carried her back up the mountain, and the whole family tended to her. It was days before she came 'round and could sip broth and water. Bless her little heart. She was scared to death and didn't trust anybody at first. Heck, I don't blame her, can you imagine a passel of kids and grownups looking down at you in great wonder? Her skin was dark, and she looked different from the rest of the family. Finally, after a while, she decided that she was among friends. Besides, she didn't have strength enough to whip a cat if she had wanted to get out of there. Weakness and starvation have a way of making a person more sensible. She was a Christian woman, and they assured her that the Cook, Meade, and Jewell families were also God fearing people. They read the Bible at her bed side every day that she was bed bound. She liked that. She mended quickly with grandmother's tonics and poultices, but she still had nightmares about her past.

"Little Sulie stayed there living and helping them just like family, for about eighteen to twenty months, or so. This was the first time any of them had seen a Nubian woman, but they had read about them in the Bible. It was in some of the first journals, it seemed the English court had black slaves and my ancestors had seen them. Great-grandma swore that Sulie was from the Lost Tribe of Israel, and thought of her as a holy person. She wrote that Sulie's skin was the color of fine polished mahogany, and it would glow by the firelight. Her fingers were long and her hands were beautiful. Her back and legs were scarred by the beatings a harsh master gave her, but her memories of her past were scarred deeper. She wore two large braids of hair that wrapped around her head and looked like strong ropes made of silk. They never saw her hair down after she got well. Sulie's eyes were big and looked like two shiny pieces of coal. Her teeth were as close to perfect as one had ever seen, and when she grinned, she brightened up the place where she stood. She sang songs that her mother had taught her in her native tongue. She sang all the time. Sulie would sing as she gathered eggs, or while she was sewing or anything that kept her busy. She was extremely clean and bathed regularly.

"She made herself a pallet on the floor by the fireplace, and would quickly pick it up and put it in the corner in a basket she had made, before anyone would get up. That little girl learned to cook and sew as good as my great grandma. She also learned to play the fiddle thanks to my great grandpaw and his oldest boy. Little Sulie made a beautiful instrument from a dried gourd and strung it up and played it with the greatest of ease. She added to the evening music playing and she enjoyed herself immensely. Sulie took to Irish and Scots music like a duck to water. Playing and singing came as naturally to Sulie as breathing. She celebrated life, and prayed with a joyous song and great spirit. She loved to sing religious songs. The joyous heart and soul of Sulie only convinced Grandma little Sulie was a messenger of God."

We all were under Ida Mae's power as she continued with her magic spell. She took her time and started again.

"In the beginning, little Sulie was shy and very quiet, but that was because she was in a strange place, and was never taught anything, and had bad things happen to her. Grandma figured that little Sulie was close to thirteen or fourteen. Sulie started gaining confidence and self-assurance when she learned how to do things for herself. The family taught her to read and write her name. She learned quickly, and loved to read the scriptures. She was a big help in putting food up for the winter, and helpin' in the gathering of wood. Little Sulie was very good with animals, and she loved to gather eggs in the morning. Grandma wrote that Sulie was a house slave and didn't know anything about the outdoors, other than the shack she lived in with her mother and two sisters, whom Sulie never saw again.

Ida Mae talked more about Sulie. "Little Sulie told the family about slavery, and the great war, and how the young black people had been hunted down by her own kind and sold to white slavers, and then taken by ship across the big ocean and sold to whomever could pay the price. Her family had started out serving a wealthy family on an Island before they got to the mainland. Then her family was sold to a plantation in Virginia. She was one of the lucky ones because she had not been sold away from her mother and her sisters. The slave owners were like those of the Bible, like Pharaoh and the Israelites. When God set his people free, that should have been the end of slavery. Some of the slave owners, she said, were not so bad, like the big man on the Island, but there were some that were mean and heartless, like Sulie's master in Virginia. We did not uphold slavery or any ideas like that. It was against everything we learned in the Bible. The whole clan became very protective of Sulie, as she had become like one of the family, and the family became even more convinced of the evils of slavery after they were educated by Sulie and heard her whole story.

"Sulie was at that time the only real outsider the family allowed up on the mountain. It was hard for Sulie to understand that the family did not know much about the goings on in the rest of the country, but she eventually understood the secrecy and found up here to be a safe place to live and grow. All the families loved her. Our Indian friends liked Sulie too, and she seemed to find comfort in knowing other people that were almost as dark as she was, and she loved their music as well. She loved their drums and the way they would chant. They honored her and taught her many Indian customs, like cooking different foods, and their ways of healing from the forest and from the spirit world. Sulie was like you young students, in the way that you like learning. She hungered to learn new things about the forest and about just living differently. The only thing different is, Sulie had to learn to survive the rest of her life. You learn to enhance your life by learning from your mistakes, or the mistakes made by others. Sulie didn't have that opportunity when she was young. She was like a little sheep, just doing what she was told with no thought of her own, no thought of her family, or family ties."

Learning, yearning, as freedom calls...

"Great grandma and great grandpaw taught Sulie all about the woods and how to survive it alone. She learned how to fish, and how to look for edible roots and greens, and how to find wild honey trees, and to find medicine in the woods that the clan used every day. The family gave back the gift of knowledge of the mountains that they had been given all those years ago by the Indians. It was only right that they helped her. She would not be a threat to them, especially since great grandma saw her as a walking miracle from God. Those miracles are far and few between.

"Sulie could make a shelter faster than some of the Indians up here could. She learned to hunt and use a bow and arrow, just like those Indians. She helped to bring in rabbits, squirrels, turkeys, and quail. She liked to wear moccasins like the Indians as well. Little Sulie learned mountain ways and mountain critters, which made her a stronger person. In the beginning Sulie was afraid of everything. She did not like bugs or critters of any kind. However, she learned that life was full of critters, and God made everything under the sun. Sulie was not afraid anymore. Sulie had a pressing dream of heading up north to a place where she never had to look over her shoulder.

"She waited 'til the winter was just over with, and hoped that those chasing her had forgotten all about her by that time. Leaving during rainy part of spring makes traveling a little bothersome, but it keeps a human scent down and makes you way harder to track when the rain washes the prints away. The family sadly packed Sulie up a sack with biscuits, boiled eggs, hard tack, and some honey, along with salt pork. They made a strap for her gourd instrument and strapped it to her back, gave her a long hunting knife with some flints, and taught her to stay on the ridge tops in which she was to travel, and how to travel north. Uncle Elbert, the one that brought her in, hand carved a walking staff for her and taught her how to use it against any wild beast on four or two legs. The Indians made her two pairs of strong moccasins and leggings to wear, and she had skins rolled up to use to keep her warm, or to make new clothing during her trip. She was given a bow and quiver full of arrows that strapped to her back. They also gave her charms to keep away evil. One of the boys gave her one of the best-hunting dogs to go with her; it had taken a shine to her anyway.

"The menfolk told her to stay high on the ridges, so she could see what was going on below her and no one could sneak up on her. She had been taught about the weather signs, and how to follow the stars, and the shadows of the sun in direction. With what she learned from the Indians and us, everyone knew she would be all right. She cried and hugged everyone goodbye and off she took up that mountain path and looked back only once. Everybody cried.

"It was written in three or four journals that the women folk were greatly saddened by her leaving, and also written there that the family was quiet for a week after her leaving, as if in mourning. They never heard from little Sulie again. They hoped and prayed that she made her destination, and was not caught by those southern planters looking for her. She had been added to the evening prayers for years after that. I still have a quilt that Sulie made with my grandmother. Their names are sewed in down at the bottom corner of it, as well as the date. I also have a few charcoal drawings of her that were drawn by old uncle, Charles."

She stopped for a minute or two, and we checked our recorders again and changed tapes, and turned pages in our notebooks.

One of the boys from a West Virginia college asked, "Ida Mae, had Sulie's family ever tried to get in touch with you before now?"

She said thinking, "I do not think so, honey, I think her family just found those papers that Sulie had written, like my family had taught her to do, and they read them and put together the puzzle pieces. I think they just found out where Slip Creek, West Virginia was, and after the newspapers got a hold of the story, and the television people got a hold of it, it just sort of snowballed. All those news people swarmed up here like a bunch of locusts, and that is when I told them I would only talk to students of American and Appalachian History. I told them not to come back up here unless they want to be shot. My menfolk came out and stood by me...guess that was message enough. If I was going to have to open up and talk about this stuff, I think the young people ought to have first dibs on the story," she said chuckling.

She was so pleased that we were there on her porch. She just beamed with pride as she said, "Jenny told me about a month ago that she had heard that Sulie made it to where she needed to be, and had a family up north. She had many children and great-grandchildren, whom are very proud of her and her memory. You know, Sulie wrote daily journals too. I heard from that television man that little Sulie had gone and got herself college educated. I am sure my ancestors are happy in the knowledge she was safe. I did get a letter just last week from Sulie's family. It was such a nice letter, and they are coming here next Sunday to meet with us all."

My editor had already told me that the *Bluefield Newspaper* and maybe even *The Charleston Gazette* had reported that the family of the slave girl wanted to reconnect with the Jewell's, the Meade's, and the Cooks, and they were coming to the area to meet the families. So, it was all arranged that they would meet next coming Sunday, at the Methodist Church, up on Slip Creek.

Ida Mae continued, "The women of the Methodist church down the mountain want to have a church supper in our honor. Sulie's family is coming here next Sunday down at the church, and we are all going to get together, along with all my kin and friends of the family. I guess all those city folks from the newspapers and television want to come with their cameras. Sulie's family is bringing pictures of their whole family, and I am bringing pictures of all my clan down there, and we can swap family stories and all of us can eat together. I just love church suppers," she said, as if we were not there.

She beamed with pride, and said she just couldn't wait for everybody to be under one roof and meet each other. You could see the excitement in her eyes, as those blue eyes twinkled more than they did a few minutes before.

She continued talking to all of us as if talking to a neighbor. She did not mind the flash from my camera. She did look and smile in a pose for me several times. She spoke again in a sort of daydream way, soft and looking out at the magnificent mountain view.

"We kept it a secret about helping Sulie for many years. Sulie made them promise never to tell. We never really knew then about the trouble with blacks and whites. However later, we had to be careful after we found out by a traveling preacher what was going on with the people. We found out that people did not take to helping black people too well, and if they knew you helped a black person, you could have been arrested and hung, or they would burn you out or shoot your kin, so we just kept the secret to ourselves until now.

"The whole family knew about the stories of the young African woman who came into the mountains to escape being killed by white men. As far as I know, there has never been another African person up here. Guess she was special. She was only a young teenager when they found her. How brave little Sulie must have been, and how strong she had to be to run through the thickets, climb rock cliffs, and cross creeks, and never stop until she finally just gave out and gave up, poor little thing. You know, those men that were hunting her, I believe just gave up on her because they thought she was helpless and didn't know squat about how to survive the wilderness. She was frightened out of her mind, I guess, and ran on pure fear. Funny when you think about it, being a house slave and not knowing anything about the outside world at that time is probably what saved her." Ida Mae sat back with a smile on her face that looked a lot like pride. She took a deep breath and started again.

"I can't wait to see other pictures of her. You know I have that charcoal drawing of her that we cherish dearly. I want to hear every story about her and her family. Guess they are just as curious about my family as I am about theirs. I hope they don't think I am one of those white people that have a prejudice against black people. That would just break my heart. Would you all like to see the charcoal drawings of Sulie?"

"Oh Yes!" we all chimed in.

Ida Mae stood up quickly and put her hand to the side of her mouth and shouted towards the screen door. "Jenny, hey Jenny, would you bring

out the picture of Sulie, so they can see how she looked?"

Jenny brought out a box and opened it for Ida Mae. She held up the picture protected by a class frame. It looked like it had been drawn the day before. The lines in her face were beautiful, and she looked so lifelike. It was drawn so correctly by Ida Mae's great uncle, who had never had an art lesson in his life. It looked like it might have been drawn by a renaissance artist.

We all studied the picture for at least thirty minutes, discussing and admiring the artwork. Ida's description was right on the money. Little Sulie was beautiful. Her bone structure was sharp, and she had piercing eyes, and the thick rope of braid around her head looked like a crown on the head of an ancient African queen. She looked very young, and her smile was almost like the same smile that Mona Lisa has. It was a smile of knowing.

Ida Mae looked at all of us as we were gushing over the pictures and said to us, "You know, I think I will give these pictures of Sulie to her grandchildren, as well as the quilt she and grandma made. I am glad my family saved that little girl. That just put stars into their crowns, now didn't it?" Ida sat back in the chair and started to rock and think of her next statement. She finally spoke up and jarred us a little.

"You know, we were so far back in the woods that no one at that time even noticed we were here. The terrible Civil War came and went without hardly a notice. Not a Yankee nor Rebel came to disturb our paradise. After the war, some people travelin' from up north down to the south, passed by the flat land by the river and asked a bunch of questions about the people of the mountain; they were fairly warned, and they rode on. That's about as close to the Civil War as we ever got. I must admit, in one journal, a hunting party of my family watched from a hidden place, a group of men riding along the creek bed in single file. They did not stop for long, just to water their horses and fill their canteens, and they did not attempt to go up on the mountain. My family watched them for over an hour as they looked around, and all finally rode out of sight. My kin watched them because they didn't know if they were the white slave owners that were looking for little Sulie or not. They didn't know at the time what a white slave trader looked like. The reason they watched them out of sight was to make sure they didn't go in her direction of escape.

"Another time, a couple of my uncles reported that, while hunting, they thought they heard gunfire but could not tell in which direction it was coming from because of all the mountains, sound like that echoes and bounces off the rock cliffs, and all the game had scattered in every direction. They believed it to be a skirmish of some kind. After the shooting stopped, they waited for a couple of hours before they carefully walked over and around the ridge where all the commotion was and looked down at a dozen or so bodies lying dead in the valley. Everyone else had ridden off, so they went down and gathered what horses were left that had not ran, and brought back guns and ammunition, along with other things that were left. They rode back around through the river, so they would not leave prints. I still have a couple of canteens, some swords, and the guns are put up in the attic, and we still have a couple of the saddles that we kept oiled and nice."

Ida Mae started rocking again and thinking about her past; she looked around at us smiling. She said as if it had just come to her, "You all have to come to the church next Sunday and meet Sulie's kin folk. That way, you will have another part of my story."

We just nodded again, as we were all magically entranced by this wrinkled, old, mountain woman that had lived and kept alive her unbelievable inheritance.

A time to get, a time to lose;
a time to keep, and a time to cast away.
Ecclesiastes 3:6 King James Version (KJV)

Chapter XII

Sherman William Cook was my Last Love

Reckon since I told you all about Wally, I guess you are wantin' to know who I ended up with, don't you," Ida said with a little half smile.

"Yes! Ida Mae, please tell us the story of your husband, right from the start," said Clarissa Hagerman from the University of Virginia, a petite strawberry blonde, with big brown eyes, who was at the age when everything was romantic. I could tell the way Ida Mae looked at her, she liked that age, and remembered.

She looked at us all, and with a slight smile on her face, continued with her story. "After a year and a half of mourning for my sweet Wally, I guess I was just a little bored with my life and let my guard down one Saturday while riding down the mountain on my daddy's best workhorse, looking for ginseng. I could see a figure riding across my uncle's lower meadow on the fastest horse I had ever seen. I knew by the way the person sat in the saddle, he had to be one of ours, he was glued to that saddle and he kept his head down just like our family trait. From where I was sitting, he looked like he had very long legs and a very long body. His hair was as black as the big horse he was riding. I watched him ride clean across the meadow and jump the fence with the grace of a deer. I kicked the sides of my horse and rode down the hollow rode as fast as the workhorse could go. I looked left and right for the mysterious rider, but he just disappeared. I rode down the road a good mile or so and still not a sign of him, not even dust. I rode down almost every day to see if I could get a glimpse of him, only to see the rear end of his horse jump over the fence. That horse was fast. All that boy did at that time was fuel my curiosity and my fantasies. I knew I had to meet the mysterious horsemen, but I just didn't know how. How do you stop a hurricane and introduce yourself," she laughed out loud, with all of us.

It sounded like something we all had done, like trying to meet some girl or someone that was untouchable. I had experienced that same feeling with a journalism student just this year. I could not get a time to speak to her, and she was always running out of the room.

Ida Mae rocked a little faster and smiled a little bigger, as she continued her story. "While riding back up the hollow one day, I spied a black horse tied to the willow next to the big part of the stream. I rode up slowly, not knowing who the intruder was, and looked around, when I heard, 'Well, Ida Mae, get down and come on over!'

"The voice sounded somewhat familiar, and I slid off Moses and tied him up real good, and walked through the willow branches. There sitting on a rock was Sherman Cook. You could have knocked me over with a slight breeze. He looked so different. Had it been that long since I had seen him? Had I ever seen him? He lived just over the mountain. Naturally, he was from one of the families that came over with my family. We all were close, but I guess I just didn't pay that much attention. He was right under my nose the whole time. But, you know how young boys are, with all the hunting and fishing, and going their own way, and me being a young girl with all the cooking and sewing, and still mourning Wally; I just didn't even think of other boys that way. Could I have been that busy?

"Anyway, here was this ruggedly handsome young man, with hair black as a moonless night and eyes as blue as any Robin's egg. He was about as handsome a man as I had ever seen. His body was tanned from working in the fields and riding shirtless with the wind in his face. My God, he was the most beautiful human being I had ever seen in my life. He grinned as I walked closer to him. I guess the look of shock on my face was a little funny. 'Sherman Cook, is that you,' I said as the fact came to me. He laughed a little with his deepened voice and invited me to sit down and talk. We caught up with the families' news and talked about all the young people our age, and some older and some younger. A lot of things he said were lost because I kept looking at those beautiful, white teeth, and his flawless face, and the black curl that lay on his forehead. I looked at his hands and his muscled arms, and found it hard to concentrate on everything he was saying. I was smitten. It seemed just a few minutes had gone by, but when we decided to say goodbye, hours had passed. Such sweet hours. He wanted to come by the house, and I said it would be just fine. I rode back up the mountain in a daze. I told my mother and daddy about him, and they were silently relieved that I had stopped mourning for Wally, and found someone of interest from the mountain, especially from the Cook family. It was always thought, planned, and wished that the families, Jewell, Meade, and Cook would stay together.

"There was a bond with the families from the very beginning, and that still holds true. God knows, that each generation of these families had many children, the least were ten children in the Edward Jewell family, and the most were eighteen children in the Daniel Meade family, so we could pick mates without inner breedin'. Some did marry into the mountain Indians, which made a bunch of beautiful people, with beautiful skin and dark, thick hair. Of course, a few ventured off the mountain and found mates down in the flatlands, but they never broke the rule of secrecy about the mountain and what was up there, and some came back to live up here. So you see, we could marry almost anybody up on the mountain, when we got to be marrying age."

Blessings of the mountains...

"It was the secret that our ancestors swore to each other and taught everyone born after, that the location of our little paradise would never be told. Naturally, time changed a lot of that promise. It was that secret that kept us as we were and are. We were separate from the rest of the world for hundreds of years. It kept us safe and untouched, and back then, it was a good thing, but since 1890, the world started to change so quickly we couldn't hide anymore. We had to pay for the land we owned, and we had to mend the fences to keep mine speculators off the mountain, and squatters and hunters off too. We started to trade more and more down at the general store and the company store in the little town about ten miles down to the flatlands. Little townships were being formed along the Big Sandy River. Lord, I remember how that river would flood come spring. We heard terrible stories about what a flood would do, but I never experienced a flood in my life. That's one good thing I guess, living up in the mountains. Sure, we had cloudbursts, but all they did was wash out the pass every spring and fall. Sometimes we would have landslides, and they were bothersome, but I don't think we ever lost any lives or anything else because of them. Now sometimes it would get a little dry up here, but the wells and springs were good enough. We were truly blessed up here, and we are still being blessed, every day. You know, even in the dry times, it would rain on the top of the mountains.

"I know, I know, you think I am wandering away from the subject, but I had to paint the picture for you all so you would understand. It was during one of those washouts that I really got to know and fell in love with Sherman Cook. We had visited together for a few months at my house, and my family would occasionally visit his family's house, so we got to see each other quite a bit. On this one rare occasion, we got some alone time. We were riding together through the woods down near the bottom of the mountain early one morning in the spring. We had a picnic down in the strawberry hill meadow. Now mind you, there was not any monkey business, but there was a lot of tension you might say. We had picked a bucket full of wild strawberries, and a large poke full of ginseng plants so we could replant them up by the farm, and we were ready to head on back up the mountain when we noticed the wind picking up and the silverback sides of leaves from all the trees. That was a sure sign of rain. We saw the dark clouds rolling toward the mountain, and we picked up the pace of our horses. A few minutes passed until we were in a doozy of a downpour. It got harder to see, and the mud was running off the path. I was getting a little worried, and so were the horses. Sherman thought it safe to put up in a cave just off the path.

"The cave was big enough for us and the horses, and the strawberries. We found a dry spot and watched the storm for hours. There was lightning strikes all around us, and trees were falling, and the wind whipped around like a hurricane. But, I was safe as long as he was there to hold me. We talked about everything we knew and ate the strawberries. He kissed me while the rain poured down, and brothers and sisters, you can bet the farm; I kissed him back. After the rain stopped, we left the cave and tried to go back up the mountain through the mist, the steam, and the mud. We had to dismount and walk the horses up and around another way that only the youngin's knew about. It was rough going I tell you. We didn't get home until dark. The family was so glad to see us alive; no one questioned us being alone together. Some of the high winds tore down limbs from a lot of trees up on the mountain and did some damage to a couple of outbuildings. No one could see what the storm did to me and Sherman. There was a storm all right, a storm so strong that it bound our souls together forever, and we both knew we couldn't wait too much longer for the preacher. We were married about a month later, by a circuit preacher. After that, I never minded the rain at all. Yes, I was a virgin when I married Sherman. He was not, and he apologized for that, but that was ok. I guess it was better to have somebody that knew what to do.

"We were married in 1887. I was almost eighteen years old. We worked together side by side for sixty years, and those were the best years of my life. He was an excellent father and provider. He completed me, and I completed him. Where you saw one, the other was nearby. We were a true pair. Like my father, there wasn't a thing Sherman could not do. We always had more than enough, and we helped all the families that didn't have as much as we did. He was the one who extended the cemetery and built up the walls of stone to the beautiful walls that we have today up there. He made the little path wider and more accessible than it was, and he carved out many a headstone of slate to replace the ones that the weather and time had taken. He had strong family pride, as I do. He also could doctor any animal. He was indeed a gift from God to the mountain and her inhabitants. He devoted his life to making my life incredible, and helping everyone he could. He helped plow fields, he helped dig many a grave and helped bury most of my relatives, and his own children. He was strong-minded and strong bodied. He always went to church and camp meetings, and was a God-fearing man.

Sherman loved my daddy and my mamma, and we all lived together in perfect harmony. He was never too tired to help me or anyone else, or was never too tired to play with his babies and all the rest of the children up here on the mountain.

"Now, I am not sayin' that he was perfect. I had to guide him from time to time. My daddy and mamma were good teachers. We did have our little spats, but they were over by bedtime, and he always kissed me goodnight, and he kissed me goodbye and hello. We never fought at the eating table, and we never had a cross word or look in front of the children or any member of the family. He did not carry tells of personal business, and he always held me in the highest esteem. I worshiped the ground he walked on. It was my sweet Sherman who built the new additions to the cabin and made it this big. He and my daddy rebuilt all the outbuildings, and rebuilt the spring house and the long porch that you all are sitting on right now.

"By learning from my daddy, Sherman could double a dollar just by puttin' it in his hand. He was a thinker, a planner, and a problem solver. I swear, that man could make anything and grow anything. His love of horses continued until the day he died. We always had several good blooded horses he would show and race. He made a small fortune in breeding and doctoring horses, along with shoeing every horse in the county. He took over the farm when my daddy died, and kept it with the love that my daddy had. He was handed the torch of our family pride, and always kept it burning. We never sold one piece of land or our mineral rights. God supplied our needs, so we would not have to sell an inch of our land or the timber.

"He was a good father and played down on the floor with his little children. There was many a time he would go check on his cattle or horses with a child on his shoulders and one by the hand. He also sang in the church and taught Bible School. You know, he was so kind to my parents, and that made life so much easier for me and better for my parents.

"When Sherman was a young man, he fell off a horse during a jump, and was knocked unconscious for three days. After he recovered from his injury, he had occasional headaches that would put him in the bed in a darkened room. He suffered terribly with those headaches. In the early part of 1947, he had more than a usual number of headaches. We took him to a doctor in Welch, West Virginia. The doctor told us that Sherman had scar tissue that was causing his pain. He wanted to make an appointment for Sherman to visit a doctor in Charleston, West Virginia, but Sherman said he would not go that far from the house.

"My sweet Sherman died that winter of 1947 in our bed, and I was laying there with him, holding his hand. We prayed together and recited our vows of love and devotion again just for us. We kissed one last kiss, and we held each other, and he just closed his eyes and went to God. I have been here, without him ever since. I have asked the Lord to take me, so I could be with my love again, but God in his wisdom, has let me carry on until the time is right for my Savior to call me home. I think of my sweet Sherman every day, especially when it rains, and I remember the day in the old cave down at the foot of the mountain, and I think of him every time I eat wild strawberries, and every time I close my eyes to sleep."

✳✳✳✳✳✳✳✳✳✳✳✳Chapter XIII✳✳✳✳✳✳✳✳✳✳✳✳

The Twentieth Century Upon the Mountain

A ll of us upon that porch had just been in a dream type of time machine. She adjusted herself again and continued.

"Well, let's get on with my story. The beginning of the twentieth century made me realize that the world was getting smaller. It was the little things that changed me, of course, I call them little things now. Lord have mercy, I cannot imagine doing things now like we did when I was growing up. Now, don't you kids think that I am getting up above my raisin'. I still appreciate the benefits of the harder work we had to do, but, I also appreciate the minds of the twentieth century that invented convenience. I think it is just wonderful, but I didn't exactly fit into every one of those new-fangled ideas. Sherman was not impressed by the new machines. I still have my clothes line outside that I use for six or eight months out of the year. One of my sons bought me a clothes dryer and a washing machine. I still own the ringer washing machine that Sherman bought me, and I have it out back on the summer kitchen porch. Yes, I still use it from time to time, just to keep me grounded, I guess. Somebody bought me a mixer, but I rarely use it. It is very hard for me to totally depend on something new. I guess that old saying about teaching an old dog new tricks is an impossible task rings true, doesn't it?

"I remember the first electricity lines put up on the mountain. It took those linemen over six months to put up the poles and cut their way all the way up to the house. We would not have had it if it had not been for Mr. Pendry at the store down on the river. The store had it and we were just fascinated that a little glass jar could light up the evening. Mr. Pendry even had a gadget that fanned the air in the building. It truly was a marvel. Seemed that people all over the world was electrified, except us. The first place Sherman strung a wire was to the barn. Sherman said he wanted to see which cow he milked in the morning, and he didn't want to step on a chicken or a snake. It made perfectly good sense to me. One of Sherman's friends that worked down at the mine, came up and wired the house so we could have 'juice' in every room. When we got electricity in our house, it was such a blessin' to go and check on the sleeping babies without lighting a candle or an oil lamp, we just turned the switch and we could see the whole room. The twentieth century was truly the awakening in my life and my family's. Usually, at dark, we all went to bed. Mostly because pa said we had to, but also it saved the oil, and the dim light from the lamps and the fire place made poor light to read. When we read the Bible in the evenings before bed, it had to be done before darkness fell. Now, we could read the Bible after all the chores and we weren't rushing around getting things done before the reading.

"That feller that wired the house and the barn got electrocuted about a year after that, down at the mines. Seems to me his name was Woodrow Cooper, I believe, anyways, he was standing in a little bit of water and touched a wire and it blowed his head clean off."

Wanting to go on to more pleasant subject matter I am sure, one of the girls asked, "Ida Mae, what did you all do for other recreation, you know, just to get your minds off the hard times? Like, we have our television and drive-ins to give us some relief, did you have anything?"

Turn your Radio On...

While she was smiling, she said to us all, "Let me tell you about our very first radio. I told you about us getting electricity? Well, about a month after we got hooked up, Sherman had to go to the store and report on his electricity, 'juice' they called it, and when he came home, he had a wondrous box under his arm. He carried it into the house and plugged it up and turned the little knob. An amber light started to glow in the front. It had a little hum to it. Sherman said it had to warm up before it would work. Finally, after 'warming up,' another little glow was coming from the inside, and music and voices came from the wondrous box.

"We had the first radio up on the mountain, and in the early evening all the family would come to our house to listen to the radio in the front room. The adults used every chair in the house, and the kids sat in the floor in a semi-circle. Sherman put the radio on the table Daddy built, and it was like a sacred thing. No one was to put their hands on Sherman's radio. We heard mountain music and mountain gospel music come from the radio. We were all sure that God wanted us to have that radio. We heard preachers preachin' their sermons to all the sick and shut-ins, and it was decided that it was a good thing. Soon, we found a station that told stories, and we all listened intensely to those 'soap operas' as they were called. Momma and Daddy loved listenin' to it, and getting the family all together to listen to the stories on the radio.

"One evening, we had all the family over and we listened to a story on the radio. Not a word was said. I don't even remember the story, but all I know is that someone screamed on the program and a shot rang out, and grandma and grandpaw jumped up and held each other. Grandma had to be put to bed because she almost fainted, and Grandpaw came back in after tending to her smelling like liquor. One if the aunts had to go home because she wet herself." Ida Mae laughed so hard, but it was hard to tell who was laughing the hardest. We all were rolling all over the place with laughter.

Ida Mae spoke again after wiping the tears of laughter from her cheeks and said, "I just can't begin to tell you how much fun we had listening to the different programs.

"Suddenly, we had a connection to the outside world without facing strangers. In one way, it was like inviting these people into your home and letting them tell you all about the world and what was happening in it. We learned about stuff you could go and buy at the store. We learned how the weather was going to be that day and the next day, and when to cut hay or not. We learned from the farm report what the current price was on seed, and when to plant, and how we should plow to keep our top soil, and how to sell beef cattle and sheep. We became educated in how to run a better farm, and how to bake a different chocolate cake.

"The radio became the farmer's and homemaker's best friend. When we weren't learning how to do things easier and better than before, we listened to the music. The music we heard in the living room came from those big city ball rooms up in New York, Baltimore, and even in Charleston; those wonderful country sounds came from our local stations, like WELC that was in Welch, or WHIS that was in Bluefield, or even stations as far away as Nashville and somewhere in Kentucky. Even now, it seems that I like radio a lot more than television. At least with radio, I got to use my own imagination, and with television, everything is there and the faces that go with the voices are not as grand as the faces that I imagined. The radio let you imagine the sets of the stage. I knew every villain by the sound of their voices. Television shows you what the villain is supposed to look like. I don't like that. I have more channels on the radio than I have on the television anyways."

"I know what you mean Ida Mae" said Larry Conley, the blond guy. "At least I can take my radio everywhere I go, and it is small enough to fit in my jacket pocket. I have my special stations I listen to at night, like "WOWO" in Fort Wayne Indiana."

"You mean you listen to a station as far away as Fort Wayne Indiana? Why?" Ida Mae asked in complete surprise.

" Oh, Miss Ida Mae, because it is the best rockin' station at night, and the D.J they call 'Wolf Man Jack' is the greatest!" Larry Conley said, and we all agreed with him.

"I am glad you all listen to the radio; it makes you think, doesn't it ?" she said smiling.

Larry, the blonde-haired guy, set straight up and answered, "Oh yes, I think about dances and my girlfriend, and sometimes, I think about summertime at the lake or at the pool with the jukebox."

Ida Mae sat back and smiled at Larry. "So, then electricity was something very life changing for all of us. I did without it for half of my life, and you young people have had it all of yours. Can you imagine living without it?"

We all looked at each other, and shook our heads but even then, I wondered if it would be so bad.

She thought a minute and smiled and said, "Even thinking about it now,

I do believe that Daddy and Sherman were the ones that liked the electricity the most. They could lengthen their days by milking early, and listening to the radio at night while rocking in those old rocking chairs, and having some peace and quiet long after the children were in bed. That was their time."

"Sometimes Sherman would take the radio through the window and he sat out on the porch and rocked, smoked, and listened to farm reports and gospel music. But he knew he had to share, because Momma and I liked to quilt and snap beans while listening to love stories.

"The radio also brought us sad news. The local funeral homes would have an obituary program, which was followed by sweet religious music that suited the occasion. We didn't get a local paper, so that is how we found the local news about who died, and what was going on at the court house." She looked around to see who was listening. Of course, we all were listening intently!

"The radio became an important tool up here on this farm. It was the open door to the outside world that we would use to go in and out of from time to time." Ida Mae got up from her chair and slowly walked toward the far end of the porch. We watched every move she made and wondered what she was doing. She grimaced and said her hips hurt her, and sometimes her legs would tingle and would go numb. She told us that she had to walk off the pain a lot of times.

"I bet the weather reports from the local stations helped you guys a lot up here, huh," questioned Delbert Puckett from Beckley.

She turned in her walk about and said with a sly grin, "Honey, I know the weather before they do. We all did. We just had to go out on the porch and look over to yonder mountains and watch the mist or the types of clouds passin' by, or the birds or insects, or even by looking at the leaves on the leafy trees and bushes. They all will tell you what the weather's going to be. I never relied on a radio for that news," she said as she walked back to her chair to rest.

Ida Mae sat back and looked around at the funny scene, and how all the students were smiling and writing feverishly, and watched as they put new tapes into their recorders and as some changed batteries. She waited and was ready for the next group of questions.

Chapter XIV

The Turbulent Times of Worry

I know your family did not fight in the Civil War, but did any of your men go to war at all," asked Sharon Harman from the University of Virginia.

The mood quickly changed for Ida Mae as she said, "Well honey, we tried to avoid anything that had to do with the outside world, and especially with anything that could get us killed. Thank God, if grandpaw and the older ones knew about the war, they kept their mouths shut. No honey, none of our precious men fought in that stupid Civil War. I know there are families from the next valley over, and some from the back side of two mountains over, who fought and lost their menfolk, but like I said, thank God, we did not. I read every history book I could get my hands on about the Civil War, and I find it hard to believe that my people escaped the trouble between the marauding bands of soldiers. Somehow, they thought they found a shorter path or a less bothersome trail around us. God undoubtedly had a hand in protecting us from those battles. There was fighting all around us within miles, but we didn't know a thing about it.

"The other wars, of course, we could not have escaped. People from the bottom land and along the river knew about us. Our luck and our privacy just wore out. We could not escape all the world's troubles anymore. Quite a few of the area's family members fought in World War I, and some came back unscathed heroes, and some came back broken, and some didn't make it back home at all. We were all thankful for those who returned. The radio that gave us so much entertainment, gave us one bitter thing, the news of the outside world. Now, the whole family became aware of the twentieth century and the changes. For the first time, we heard the voice of the president of the United States. He encouraged all U.S. citizens and patriots, or what he called all red-blooded Americans, to enlist in the armed services. My uncles went to fight in World War I, and my sons in World War II, and quite a few of my cousins. Not all of them came back, and the ones who did, were not the same. That was the price we had to pay for fooling with the outside world. I lost two brothers, about six cousins, and many close friends. It was a troubling time for all of us. During the time of the great wars, there were people down in the bottomland and down the river who didn't do so well financially, and they came up to the stores with little stamps for things. We had those stamps too, but we didn't need half the stuff they offered, so we would barter with those who needed it. Some of them came to work our fields while our young men were away. We did take care of a lot of people that would have starved. We still hunted and fished, and remembered all those old lessons that our grandfathers taught us. They came in mighty handy for us and about fifty others that benefited from our mountain knowledge.

"Throughout the depression and both wars, we made out just fine. After we got our boys back, we swore that we would not let another one go. That was a foolish promise. I now have seven grandsons in Asia fighting Communism, and about five stationed here in the states. We are not as safe as we were years ago. It did not work out that way. I guess we had to share in the hardships of our country. After all, God did bless the whole country, didn't He? So, if we wanted the blessings to continue, we had to sacrifice. Just like in the Bible. When World War I and II came, we offered up our best. God took some, but did not take all. Thank God, he only needed a few of our best, and they were such a wonderful sacrifice to Him, he decided he had taken enough from his special group. We are a large family and a close one. If we argue, we have too many peace makers around to let a feud break up our peaceful existence here on this mountain. We get our differences and squabbles over with, and go on about our business. No one person up here stays mad at someone else for any long length of time. We work hard together, we play together, we live close to each other, and our doors are always open. Now, like I said, we fix our problems, but you let one outsider come up here and pick a fight and it is like pickin' a fight with a giant swarm of hornets. In other words, you mess with one, you mess with the whole mountain. No one in their right mind would come up with ill feelings or a fight on their mind.

"You all asked me about being aware of the twentieth century. We did become aware, and we did our best to keep up, but we didn't change so much that we left our old ways of love and kinship behind. The past is far stronger than the present, and I believe sweeter than the future. You children will understand as you get older. You just can't lay down old ways. It is hard to change. Maybe change isn't worth the effort. Sure, it is fun having electric lights and television. I love listening to people talk and sing on the radio, and that is a pleasure in my old age. But what a real pleasure is to me, is having my mother's quilt on my bed, having this rocking chair that my grandpaw made, and living here in this fine cabin that my ancestors built, and my grandfather rebuilt, and my daddy added on to, and my Sherman perfected.

"Look at my fine cemetery that Sherman finished where Daddy left off. When you read the headstones and read those fine names and dates, you will understand that they were the ones who started this way of life that I am trying to carry on. These are the things that make me proud of my heritage. I can touch this, and I don't have to look at it in pictures. This is a house that was built for the first time in the seventeenth century. Yes, it looks different, yet it is the same. It is on the same spot that my great, great, great, great, great grandfather stood and chose to raise his family, and to make history. All the electricity and quick hot water in the world is not worth what I have known, what I have seen, and what I have experienced. Now I have been here maybe past my given time, but I want to make sure that when I go to glory, my legacy will be kept sacred here. My children, and their children will take care of this house, and I have a grandson who is interested in living here with his ever growin' family. He is a hunter and a fisherman, and a true lover of the mountains. This makes me proud to think of him taking care of the legacy, and my books, and wanting to learn more about his ancestors. You cannot put a price or trade on that.

"There was a time in my life that I did not communicate, nor care to, with anybody outside my mountain range, and there was a time when I carried water, and I built fires in the morning to get the house warm, and I washed clothes outside in a big tub, and I made my own soap, and I would not have dreamed of having the stuff I have now. But, I want you all to know that I would trade it all today to have the peace of mind and simple life again. We all got spoiled. Well, maybe not all of us."

She laughed a little, but we were all quiet. We didn't make a noise as we traveled forward to 'now' with her. I didn't want to break the spell. I felt older somehow. I also was thankful for my life, and how my life was simple and much easier than her young life. God, I thought, she thought life was simple then? She had to be tough. I would not have lived this long for sure. We got up and stretched again, and got fresh pens and batteries, and got our stuff in order for the next phase of her remarkable life. I wanted desperately to go home and talk to my grandmother and grandfather about anything. They would know stuff about my family and the blood that flows through my veins. Suddenly that 'corny stuff' wasn't so corny and now seemed to be very important to me. I wanted to know about ME. I wanted to talk to uncles, aunts, and old family friends. I wanted to get the scrapbooks and old school annuals out and own them and take care of them just as Ida Mae took care of her knowledge.

Chapter XV

The Cemetery

W ell, I have to tell you all about the sad times of my life. You cannot have an even balance of a sweet life, without a little bitterness. It makes a good pie," she said very solemnly.

We sat there very quiet, and we were more than ready for this story. She looked at us all right in the eye, then turned again to the view of the Blue Ridge. When she looked out over there, she seemed to gain strength and her whole demeanor changed.

I spoke up and said, "Go ahead Ida Mae, we are ready for you, honey."

She never took her eyes from the hypnotic view, and then she spoke. "Naturally, when the families reached the homestead, there was a need to find a special resting place for our honored dead. The first to die was old Ruarc Cook, at the age of 79. The families decided to bury him right on the edge of the woods and the clearing. That area hadn't been cleared all that well, but, after Ruarc died, they started clearing it off, and started burying there from then on.

"At first, the cemetery was blocked off and it contained about half an acre. When the families plowed their fields, the big stones were used for the chimneys or inside fireplaces; if there were any left-overs, they were used to make the wall of the cemetery. It seemed that God wanted the stones for that very thing, because this whole place is just full of those big stones. The original wall was only about three feet tall. There was a wooden gate that one of the Meade boys and Nathanial Cook, Rurac's son, made from the best wood around. One of the ancestors was an expert stone mason and carver, I think it was Robert and Simon Cook. They took care of the beautiful headstones. The cemetery was a sacred place to our families. Our dead were not forgotten, and there are at least ten of the journals that I have, describing everyone who lies there, and how they died, and a story or two about them. Everyone took care of the cemetery. There was not ever a patch of weeds that sprung up there or scrub trees, no sir. There used to be a large oak that used to cover and shelter the cemetery, along with some pines as witnesses. But the storm, that brought me and Sherman together, took that old tree down. There are a few pieces of furniture in my house that were made from that big old oak.

"We always had a Decoration Day. We picked flowers and placed them on the cleaned graves. We would pick up sticks and twigs that were left from storms, and make sure that all the stones were straight and tall. We brought our dinners and ate on the grounds. There were picnic tables made and placed there I think in the early 1800's, of course they have been replaced a couple of times since then. Time and weather must take its claim too.

"During the decoration celebration, we would have a preacher and some of the family elders to speak and tell stories of the family. We brought up instruments and we sang songs all day. The children would run in the adjoinin' meadow and created games to keep them occupied. You would think it would be a sad day when you go to the cemetery, but we brought the fun and life back to the cemetery, so our relatives could see that we were all in fine shape. No more sadness for them.

"Back in 1965, the menfolk built a real nice picnic shelter for all of us. When I go up there, sometimes when I am through visiting my people, I go over to the picnic shelter and sit a spell and look out over the hillside. I can sit there for hours and watch the hawks fly by, and just listen to the mountains breathe.

"I used to dread funerals. I had to go to funerals when I was young. We were not kept at home because we were little. We had to attend every one of the funerals, and we knew how to act at a funeral. We were also taught not to fear the dead of our family. I remember my grandparent's funerals, and my aunts and uncles. Those were some hard funerals to go to. When you see your momma and daddy cry over their parents, it is just heart rendering. Some years would pass when we had to only attend maybe one or two, then three or four funerals, and then some years would come when we attended ten or more. But, that's the way with big families, I guess. I don't dread the funerals as much now after I came to understand the cycle of things. 'To everything, there is a season,' that's what the Bible says."

A time to be born and a time to die...

"Of course, I remember my father's funeral. I think that is when my own mortality really hit me. Even though I was married and had children, my daddy was the center my life. He had spoiled me and was my protector all my young life, and I spoiled him in his older life. I will never forget the sight of those coal miners carrying my father up the mountain one gloomy day. He was still black from the coal dirt, and all the fellows that he worked with were walking up the hill with Daddy's body. Mother had just finished the evening dishes when she heard a scream from one of my sisters. She knew by the sound of the scream that she didn't need to rush outside.

"She had a vision of Daddy earlier, while getting the dishwater ready. She plainly saw him walking up the road with his dinner bucket in his hand and some flowers in the other. She thought he looked strange coming home so early from the mine. She watched him as he walked up to the yard, and then he faded away. Momma knew before anyone did that he had passed. My grandmother had a vision of my grand-daddy walking across the yard with flowers in his hand before being told that grand-daddy died. My mother calmly walked to the kitchen door, opened the screen door, and watched them carry my daddy up the steps into the house. I was upstairs drying one of the children and getting them dressed when I heard that scream. I ran downstairs to see them carrying my daddy. They laid him on the kitchen table. Mother fell to her knees beside of me and I held her as we rocked back and forth crying. One of the children ran over to one of the uncle's house to get them to come. The whole family was dumbstruck. Daddy had milked and fed earlier that very morning. We all assumed that Daddy wasn't too old to work in the mines, and that he would eventually die in his own bed. But, we don't have control of those things, do we?

Ida Mae continued with her memory, "The miners that brought my daddy home left as quietly as they came. Me and my sisters helped mother up and attend to our father, her husband. We gently removed his work clothing, and washed his body with the most reverent care. Mother draped his body with a towel as not to shame him in front of his daughters. I remember that there was not one mark on his body that would have caused death. He just died where he stood, I guess. Mother asked us to leave as she finished washing Daddy. We did as we were told. When we came back inside, about an hour later, mother had Daddy cleaned down to his toenails and fingernails.

Ida Mae said, "He was dressed in his only white shirt and his black church pants with his black suspenders. That was all he had. She had already put his Sunday boots on him and they had been polished. His thick, salt and pepper hair was combed neatly, and his beard had been trimmed and well groomed. He looked so handsome. I never looked at my daddy that way, but he was a handsome man for his age. One of his brothers and Sherman built his coffin that night and brought it up, and they, with the help of one of his brothers, laid Daddy in it. They put the casket on the kitchen table, and all the families were there. Friends and family had brought all kinds of food so Momma and I didn't have to cook for the crowd that gathered. She looked so tired and old that night. I never knew she had aged until that evening before we buried Daddy. Sherman and some of the brothers, and some of the miners that Daddy worked with, dug the grave by lantern light. We buried Daddy that next day. I remember that day as if it were yesterday. We all walked up the hill to the cemetery, and his brothers carried the coffin with my daddy in it on their shoulders that seemed so wide and strong. Thank God, I had my Sherman to hold on to as I remember. Poor Momma, that had to be the longest walk of her life. It was a long walk for me too, as I was pregnant with Brown at that time."

"The women folk sang mountain songs of pain and misery, and the promise of Heaven. The circuit preacher came, and the Baptist minister from down the mountain came up, and so did preacher Russ, and they preached. They knew Daddy well. We didn't get home until late that afternoon. Momma just went straight into her bedroom and closed the door. We still had plenty of food from the day before, and we ate leftovers for a couple of days. We left Momma alone for a while to let her mourn on her own. We did not know how long she would be closed off in her bedroom. I could hear her cry behind the door as I stood and cried my own tears. My heart was also broken. We waited. Two days later, I went into early labor and delivered Brown with the aid of an aunt that was a midwife, and Momma. Momma came out of her room the minute I had my first pain, with her eyes still swollen, she said we had done all we can do for the dead, now there was the tending of life to do, so we had to get on with it. And we did. She helped with everything, and made me feel better knowing I was in good hands."

"Momma went to the cemetery every day for almost a year. I went a lot of times with her, but I had a baby to watch and a family to cook for. I admired her for her devotion to her husband and her family. She never openly grieved, but her heart and her love was gone. She never was the same, although the birth of sweet little Brown seemed to come at a good time. God sure does know about timing. She seemed a little quieter and that special spark was gone out of her eyes, even when the whole family was around her. She went to church as much as she could, weather permitting, and read the Bible even more than she did before.

"Three years to the day of my father's death, Momma died in her sleep with her Bible on her chest. She hadn't even been sick, or complained about a thing. She knew that we all would be fine now that the sisters were married, and we had our families to watch after us and we would all be busy with our children, so she just willed herself to die. She wanted to quit life. She was so lost without her man. My sisters and me, along with Momma's sister that lived close by, attended to her as we did Daddy, only we dressed Momma in her bed. I combed her hair and let it rest in long waves over her shoulders. Her hair was still red, maybe a little more faded than her youthful mane, and it was mixed with a few gray strands, which seemed to be more bountiful in the last three years. Her funeral was not any different than my daddy's. We placed her beside her man, and there alongside her dead babies. Sherman made sure that we would lie beside of them later.

"Sherman and I lived in this cabin at the time of Momma's death, along with two brothers and one sister that had not married. Sherman wanted some privacy and some more room in the house, so he had built the extra four rooms attached to the back of the house, which was our living quarters, and an extra sitting room for anybody who wanted to sit and read, court, or rest. Sherman got a few of the cousins and brother-in-laws to help him roll a couple of cabins up to join on both sides of the original cabin. Elbert married and brought his wife home to live with us for a couple of years until he could clear off some land and get some money in his pocket. So, they basically had the bottom left side of the house for themselves. We all got along without one incident of temper.

"Sherman loved books and he knew that they were my passion also, so he made bookshelves all over the place and they were quickly filled. He loved to build and work with his hands. He was always doing something to keep his mind and hands busy. Only during the working days of the week did the cabin seem empty, come the weekend it had every corner filled with aunts, uncles, cousins, sisters, brothers, and their brood. There was some serious cooking and the work that goes with it during those weekends. Lordy!

"Sherman and I started filling the cabin up pretty quick. All my children were born and raised right here in this same cabin as all my ancestors were. This front part of the cabin is where Momma and Daddy first lived together and gave birth to their family. It doesn't look the same as it did then. While Momma and Daddy were still alive, we started to enlarge the cabin. Sherman was always building on the cabin. He added a small family cabin to it when we first got married. The addition made the house cooler, and we had a cabin that was built outside of the main cabin that was used for cooking. Sherman added the little cooking cabin to the back side of the kitchen for convenience and extra space for the long table. It had windows, and we closed the door during the summer months, and opened it up during the winter.

"This house became the hub of the family wheel. Whenever the family needed to get together for any special occasion, it was right here at the old home place. If they wanted to stay for whatever reason, or just to stay after we played cards, or had a late night pickin', there was always a bedroom waiting for them. We don't use the summer kitchen that much anymore, but it is left the same and is ready when needed, just in case. Like I said, the house is the center hub of our giant wheel, but our beautiful cemetery is the grease. The wheel will not work long, or not at all, if the grease isn't there. We could not have been here if not for our ancestors. The cemetery is constantly visited by one of us. We sit and meditate on the benches that Sherman built for just that purpose. We all go there to think or to pray. It will never be forgotten like other graveyards. Our cemetery is honored. The preacher likes it up here, so he comes and preaches awhile, and some of the church members come to visit and sing, and they all join in with the family from time to time. So the tradition carries on, we bury our family in our cemetery, keep it clean, and honor our glorious family sleeping there.

"We were married in the meadow beside the cemetery. We wanted to honor our family with them attending as if they were there in the flesh. I know they were there in the spirit. I could feel the presence of every one of them. Sherman didn't mind at all because he felt the same as I did; after all, they were his relatives too. The cemetery was the anchor. It kept us all grounded, and helped us all to hold on to what was ours, and why we fought so hard to keep our life the way that it is. Our legacy was there for us all to see. This was our proof of history. All our uncles, aunts, cousins of every degree, brothers, sisters, mothers, and fathers are in one place, so when the Lord calls up the dead, he won't have to look too far to find my family. We'll all be right here, together, waiting for the Trumpet's blast."

At this very time, I began to re-assess my life. My parents should've been here to listen to this story, so they could learn as I did. This is the way that life was supposed to be. What happened to us all? Why did we feel that there was a need to change anything? There wasn't a need for a supermarket, a designer clothing store, insurance, government assistance, a large bank account, four-lane highways, or even a fast food restaurant. Ida Mae's people didn't need our way of thinking. These people had their own way of worship, their own way of food preparation and preservation, their own music, their own way of uncluttered thinking, family pride, and their own work. These families did not need the 'new' world at all. I didn't feel so important anymore. When I look at their life, I feel that I have done nothing with mine. By my age, the mountain boys had already made a home for themselves, had their own work in the fields or the mines, and had a family, and they knew what they were going to do the rest of their lives. I had problems wondering what I was going to wear tomorrow, or for that matter, even where I was going to work after graduation. I hadn't a clue. Sure, I had some dreams, but God, now they all seem so stupid and petty. I was quietly thinking just as I'm sure the other kids were, and my smile had melted away. I was ashamed of myself. Her voice brought me back and gave me a jolt.

"Ya'll want something to drink or eat," she said, breaking another spell that she had put us under.

She got up and went inside the house again, and came out bringing a picture of an older man. She sat down and handed the picture to the nearest person next to her. She said calmly, "This here is the last picture taken of my sweet Sherman Cook. He's older in this picture; we had pictures made down at the church six months before he died. He was a good, honest, hardworking man, and as you can see, he was good lookin' even in his older years. He kept his promise that he would always love only me, and be a good provider. He is buried up there close to my Momma and Daddy. There is a place right next to him where I will sleep. Sherman was the one who made the cemetery such a beautiful place. He was the one that made the stone sittin' places there. I try to go up there about once a week. Lately, it has been just too hot to go up there, even though the shade of the big trees is a welcome sight. I have to have help getting up there, my knees aren't what they used to be. We can go by car up there now. The road was grated, worked, and it is very smooth travelin' up there. Why don't you young folks walk up there and look at the cemetery, and check it out for me and see if everything is ok. Would you all do that for old Ida Mae," she said tilting her head and smiling.

Traveling to the end of the road...

We all got up looked back at her, and she just pointed to her left. We knew where to go by the smooth road she described. It was not that far from the house, it was maybe two football field's length away from the main cabin. As we walked past the cabin, we noticed a young woman hanging up laundry on the clothesline behind the house. The white sheets whipped in the wind and the glare of the sun on that stark white would almost blind you. The sweet smell of freshly laundered linen blended in the breeze with the spring flowers and freshly mown grass. The walk was pleasant, and it did us all good to stretch our legs and move around a bit. Now that I think about it, we probably looked like a marching row of ants going up that little hill. We did it without question, and I would say that if she told us to go on up and jump off the cliff, my guess was, we would have done it.

The road to the cemetery led to a slightly wooded area after we passed the barn and the work sheds. The road had been graded smoothly. There was meadow on both sides of the road, and grasses of every color woven with Queen Ann's Lace and Chicory that lined the barbed wire fences, made for a beautiful walk. There were little, white butterflies and honey bees busily working the blooms. The smell of fresh cut hay and the sight of the hay bales just helped with our transportation to the past. I could see the rock wall of the cemetery from the minute that we cleared the barns. It stood right on top of a green knoll with trees around it. Alongside the cemetery was a huge picnic shelter built with logs with stone pillars, and had a cement floor and a huge stone fireplace inside it. It looked so well made and kept, that one would think they were in a state park or something like that. The whole area was shaded and stood out as a magnificent tribute to the blessed ones buried there. The walls of stone in the cemetery looked like the ones you would see in Ireland or in England, and it was at least, including the little stones on the top for decoration, five feet tall all the way around. There just off from the center, were Ida Mae's parents and Sherman's grave. It had wilted flowers laying on them. There were some flowers planted there inside the fortress, but they were very carefully and purposely planted. I don't believe that I had ever seen any flower as beautiful as those. This whole place seemed so sacred, like we were in some important church. We walked through the wonderful tall iron gate that had a slight squeak when we pulled it open. Walking carefully between the graves and reading the stones, we spoke in a respectful whisper. The little redhead stopped at a tiny grave that had a little angel sitting on the gravestone, and I watched her wipe a tear from her eyes. I can bring that memory up as if it were yesterday, and it is still so fresh in my mind that I almost cry myself. I guess we spent the better part of an hour up there. I sat on one of the stone benches that Sherman had made. I could almost feel Sherman's presence there, and feel his pride of the stone. He was a true master of stonework. I saw on the side of the stone bench the initials 'S C' and the date of 1917, carved beautifully by a loving hand. Every piece fit like puzzle pieces, and each stone was placed in by his hands and it seemed only he knew how to finish the puzzle.

Very little mortar was used in the placement of the stones, yet the stones were there to stay. The stone wall now stretched at least three and a half acres with room on both sides for expansion if there be a need. A lot of work went into this. This was the type of cemetery that you'd see in pictures of Ireland or Scotland. The gate was a piece of art in itself. He had worked that metal and made it look like ivy was entwined along the long bars of the gate. It had scrolled ivy vines working its way down the sides and along the top. The gate had a slide bolt that kept it closed until it needed to be opened. Even with all the deer up there, they never ate the flowers inside the walls. I prayed under my breath for myself and for Ida Mae and her family.

We all decided to walk back on down to the cabin. The walk back down was slower, but it was breathtaking. We were higher than the front porch of the cabin, so we got a better view of most of the land surrounding the area. We could look down on the roof of the cabin and see the handiwork of the homemade, shaker type shingles, and the four chimneys that were made of the same wonderful, light-colored stone as the cemetery. Everywhere you would look, it showed work done by a proud hand long gone. I could see a couple more cabins just around the hill, and roads leading I am sure to the other cabins of the family. Everything was so well maintained. The fences were in good shape, and the lower meadow was lush and almost ready to be cut after they finished with the upper meadows. The cattle in the field had new little calves running everywhere and they were fat as they could be, and the goats in the backfield, along with their babies, were busy watching us through the fencing. There was not that 'farmy' smell anywhere. It smelled sweet everywhere we walked.

We finally made it back on the porch, and there waiting for us were some peanut butter and jelly sandwiches. *What part of Heaven was copied for this?* My God, it was the jelly I was talking about. I just knew it! I had never tasted anything so good and comforting in my life. It occurred to me that I had never tasted homemade preserves before. I may never be the same. She served her wonderful ice tea and offered cold buttermilk, but none of us accepted the buttermilk. Sorry, I love the whole country thing, but I just cannot do the buttermilk. I can't do yogurt either.

There were more than enough sandwiches, so I ate another one. I could not help myself. Just when I thought that satisfaction had a new name, from out of the kitchen came Jenny with freshly made chocolate fudge. I was convinced that I had died and gone to Heaven right there. We were like termites. There was not a crumb left of anything. She sure knew how to take care of company.

Jenny asked us, "Well, did you young people see our cemetery that Daddy and Granddaddy made?"

We all spoke at the same time, talking about the beauty of the stone, the gate, the headstones, talking about who was where.

Ida Mae said, "I told you that you would see the pride of our family. That is why I asked for history students and Appalachian culture students. You all would appreciate this more than just someone who wanted a good story."

Everyone smiled and shook their heads in agreement with her. I felt two inches tall when she said that. It was I who thought this would be just a routine interview. It was I who thought I could whip this thing out and never even think twice about it. Now, it was I who didn't want to leave. Was it me who wanted to live like this forever? Me, the big shot at college, who hung on every word this wonderful, one hundred-year-old woman had to say, and it was I who was blessed that day. *What just happened to me?*

Ida Mae looked at me and gave me another little, funny wink and said low, "I told you so."

I guess that the look on my face told it all. She was a good face reader. She knew what I was all about, and she smiled at me and I smiled back. She had won the battle of the doubting minds. I am now a proud, Appalachian born man. I am proud of the mountains where I was born.

Chapter XVI

Going Home

Ida Mae had set there in that old wooden rocker for about an hour and a half since the last break, when she pushed herself up to her feet.

"You all just sit right there, I have to stretch my body just a bit," she said with a little grunt as she pulled herself up from the chair. She walked to the edge of the porch, put her hands on the rough wood railing, and looked out over the distance.

She said slowly and softly, "You know children, God visits here all the time," she turned her head towards us and smiled gently, then turned back to the beautiful sight.

"Do you young people see, that foggy looking stuff just around the ridges," she asked.

"It lays around the ridges all the time up here when its early morning or when it is rainy, but it makes this place smell so sweet and fresh, and the birds fly around it, but they don't fly into it because it makes their feathers wet." She seemed to be thinking back on something and then she said. "What else do you young people want to talk about?

One of the students asked, "Ms. Cook, how do you feel, I mean, how important is religion to you up here on the mountain?"

She continued without even blinking, "Oh, He has been here all along. His hand is on everything on this mountain. As I said, God visits here all the time. This is His favorite 'get away' from all that Heaven business. He likes to walk in the forest and feel the pine needles 'neath His mighty feet, and the meadow grasses bow before Him. He waves His mighty hand, and the sun brightens up even the darkest place in the woods. How could anyone not believe in God Almighty, when I have seen His footprints, and I have felt Him passing by me? Everywhere you look, God has left his calling cards, the birds, the butterflies, the inchworm, and even the littlest ladybug. These are things he has left behind to remind us that He is present. This place and all around is His church. We are supposed to be thankful for everything we see and do. I pray before each meal, before my feet touch the floor in the morning, and before I put my feet in the bed at night. If I wake up during the night, I pray before I fall back to sleep. He is always on my mind. Here I am, one hundred years old, and I still feel wonderful and proud to be alive. I have seen a lot of things come and go, and that may not mean a whole hill of beans, but God is constant and never changing. The Bible is old, but every day you can read something that has to do with life today. It is a true guide on how to live and how to die."

She moved back to the rocking chair and brushed a few stray, snow-white hairs that the breeze had moved away from her crystal blue eyes. "When I can, I go down to the church at the bottom of the road. I just love those people who go there. They all come over to me and wish me well, but they love it when we have our church suppers, and I bring the banana pudding, chicken and dumplings, and the molasses stack cakes. Lordy! Like I said before, they like to come up here every once I a while. When I can't go down to the little church, or don't have a ride, I wander on up to the cemetery and have a good talk with the Lord right there. Sometimes, I worship right here on this porch; I feel this old porch is a very holy place too."

She rocked a few times and then said, "You are wondering if I am ready to die? Yes-sir-ree, I am ready to die. I am not afraid. I am ready to die today if my Savior called me right now. I am right with the Lord, and I have lived a good long life and walked with the Lord every day," she said as if talking to herself.

Ida Mae smiled and said, "I do want a nice funeral. I really don't care about the box they put me in. I already have a nice blue dress put up in the chiffarobe for when they bury me. I want the women in the choir to sing real pretty for me, and I want the people of the church to eat a good meal right there at the church on the picnic grounds. I want to be remembered as a good woman, not just as some silly, old woman who lived a long time up here on this mountain. I want my people to be remembered. I want my kin, my children, and how we lived and survived the harshness of life to be remembered. I want people to know how we branched out our family tree about as much as you can branch out," she said proudly and continued rocking.

With a little tear in her eye she looked out over the porch and said, "I know Heaven is wonderful, but I will miss it here and miss all my kin, and I pray that our merciful God will let me visit and maybe walk with him when He comes down here to think and rest."

The young man from West Virginia University said, "Mrs. Cook because we are writing down and recording everything you have said, and your words will be published and studied by thousands of people. Your state must be extremely proud of you and your family. I can't think of anyone else I would rather read about, and I do not think you will ever be forgotten. We think you will be remembered as a Godly woman from a very good family."

She looked at him with a little tear in her eye and said to him, "Thank you, honey, that's all I wanted to hear from someone. I guess that is all a body really needs to hear just to keep going one more day."

She tilted her head over towards the students sitting on her porch and said with a slight smile, "You know, when I was young, I felt my life was like a full bucket from the well. The more I lived and learned, the more was splashed out and lost, but was constantly being replaced by time so that I would have an ever-filling bucket. But now, I have grown old and have done just about more than any person I know. I feel as if my bucket is running low, and I have done everything I could to keep it to the brim, but to no avail. I am losing the battle, and I feel as if my bucket's got a hole in it, you know? Isn't there a song called, "My Bucket's got a Hole in it," or "There's a Hole in My Bucket"... or something like that. Well, that's how I feel right now!"

Everybody chuckled along with Ida Mae as she rocked with the afternoon sun shining on her aged, wise face and glistening on her pearl-white hair. She fingered the collar of her floral blouse, and I wondered if it was getting a little warm on her. I noticed that she had left the two top buttons casually unbuttoned, displaying the freckled skin that seemed to drape from her chin to her chest. Her skin was golden, she wasn't pasty white as some old people get, and her skin appeared as soft as a newborn's skin. Her fingers were long and thin, and her fingernails were filed to just the fingertips. She wore a plain gold band, worn thin through the years, but more precious than ever.

She moved her hands as she talked as if it helped to make us understand. These were the hands of a woman who had brought life into the world and buried it. Her flesh on her hands was almost transparent, with the blue veins showing through the thin skin. She had been a planter and a harvester; she had been a lover, wife, mother, widow, grandmother, teacher and student, a mourner, a good friend, and she had been strong and weak, but always a child of the mountains.

Before we stepped off the porch, and before our last goodbye, she announced, "Now you children don't forget to come to my church this Sunday so that you can see Sulie's relatives. It should be a blessed event."

We all said we would be there as we thanked her for the informative day along with the best food I ever had. It made her happy knowing we loved being there and shared her story.

I went over to her and hugged her and told her that she could count on me to be there and I would see her soon. She smiled and said, "I know you will be there."

We all decided as we walked to our cars that day that we would be changed forever by being up there on that mountain, and having this wonderful step into the past with Ida Mae and her wonderful family that made mountain people a category all their own. We all wanted to go back and trace our own families, and find the spring that will fill all our buckets of life.

The Celebration at the Slip Creek Church of Christ

Well, I just have to tell you that I would not have missed this event for all the tea in China. I went to the church there on the mountain that Sunday. Yes, I traveled back to where the story began, only not quite so far, as the church was at the base of the big mountain. I was the only one of the other students to go. I figured it would be a follow up on my story, after all, this was a major part of the continuation of the story of Ida Mae Cook, for heaven's sake.

I followed the same route that I had driven just a week before, and found the church just down the ridge about fifteen minutes from Ida Mae's land. Ida Mae seemed so glad to see me, and she hugged me tenderly. She let me have a picture with her, and I took a great many photographs of Ida Mae with all the people who came to see the great 'homecoming.' The moment arrived when a caravan of long black cars pulled up, and fifteen or so black people came inside the little church. At first, everyone just looked curiously, and then someone started clapping, and everyone clapped and cheered. The faces on the black visitors were quickly changed from nervous to glad in just a second. Everyone in Ida Mae's family had photos placed on long tables, and on the other side of the room were tables filled to the brim with homemade, country food. You could smell chicken and dumplings and home-made bread all over that mountain.

Sulie's grandchildren and great-grandchildren all came with pictures of Sulie, her children, and her home. They even brought Sulie's diploma from a black college in Michigan and Canada. We all found out that Sulie was famous for her mysterious cures, and she became a midwife and delivered close to seven hundred babies. She could grow anything and had the best garden in the state. Sulie had studied medicine and became a licensed nurse. She married a good man, a doctor, and had nine children, and found time to write a book of her adventures. They owned a farm not far from the boarder of Canada.

Just when everybody had said about all there was to say, Ida motioned for her grandson, Riley, to bring the box that was under the table in the back of the room. Everyone got quiet as he placed the big, flat box on her lap. She untied the twine that held it closed, and brought out a beautiful old quilt. It was a little frayed on a couple of the corners, and maybe just a bit faded from hanging in the sun to dry, but the beauty and the love were obvious in every stitch. Everyone looked in amazement as she let her kids hold up the quilt. They laid it out on an empty table, so everyone could come up and walk around it, and admire the stitches, the names, and the dates.

Ida Mae stood up and addressed Sulie's family. "This here is a quilt that little Sulie and Momma and Grandma worked on while Sulie lived with my family. If you look down on the right-hand corner, it has all three of their names embroidered on it. They said that Sulie cried when the quilt was finished because she knew she didn't have time to work on another. I want you all to have this, and put it in a special place because it was made by special people. I also have a couple of charcoal drawings of Sulie that my uncle drew of her. They were framed by my son, and the wood used in the frame was from our old barn. As you can tell by the soft strokes of the charcoal, she was beautiful and was loved by my family."

Everyone had a tissue up to their eyes and noses. It was so very quiet in the church at that moment. Then, the eldest of the black men stepped forward and unwrapped a hand carved walking stick.

He held the walking stick up above his head, and said, "Miss Ida Mae, this is the walking stick that Mr. Elbert carved for my grandmother so that she could keep steady and secure during her long walk. She treasured it all the rest of her long life as if it were made of gold. It has gone through the long journey and two house fires, and it still came through unscathed. This staff represents the struggle of both our families trying to survive. She wanted this to go to your family, and made us promise that we would do that very thing. Sulie told her family that you saved a little girl's life, and you saved a whole family."

Ida Mae got up with the aid of her son, and walked over to the man and hugged him as she wept.

He wept as he held on to her and kissed her on the cheek and said, "Thank you and your blessed family. God bless your whole family and may they all live long, and keep the stories alive."

Now everyone was crying, and the preacher thought it would be a good time to pray. We all bowed our heads as he said, "Dear Heavenly Father, thank you for this exceptional day. Thank you for bringing these families together at last, and thank you for the legacy that is being remembered from years long past and for the years yet to come. We pray today for those who are struggling now and will in the future, may you grant them peace and comfort as you have done here today. Thank you, Lord, for the love of the people, and for this land in which we all live. We pray for world peace, and for bringing more brothers and sisters to you. In Jesus name, we pray, Amen."

It was still quiet after the "Amens," and then the preacher said loudly, "Let's all eat before it gets cold!"

Everyone stood up and, like little soldiers, formed two lines that went straight to the long tables. Waiting in line until they finally got a plate, each person filled it full and went outside and sat at picnic tables set out on the grass beside the church. The food table seemed to be restocked every five minutes. I went back for seconds and thirds, and the menu had changed every time I went back. I thought to myself, the church women up here on this mountain could sure teach our ladies in the cafeteria at school a few tricks. Even now, I still think of that spread, and my mouth will start to water.

I left again off that mountain when the sun was starting to set with a full belly, a full mind, a full bag of food wrapped in aluminum foil, and a full heart. And again, I was the last to leave. It was the ending of a perfectly beautiful, storybook day. Everyone left about the same time, and what wasn't eaten was taken out of the church basement by church members in aluminum foil bundles. Ida left with her walking staff, and Sulie's family left with the treasured quilt only after exchanging addresses, phone numbers, and hugs and kisses. Something wonderful happened that day, and I witnessed it.

I did what I set out to do, and I did it well. I knew my life would never be the same. I arrived on that mountain a silly, self-centered boy, and left there an educated, thoughtful man.

~ ~ ~ ~ **TIME** ~ ~ ~ ~

Now, it has come to this particular time in my life when I can, with a pleasant emotion, think back. I did get the "A" on my coveted interview, and my editor gave it to the *Bluefield Daily Telegraph* and the *Charleston Gazette*. I was the only student there to go that extra mile and push and promote my story.

I sold my pictures to *Life Magazine*, and my story was purchased separately. I made enough money to pay for grad school, and to help me get a start in life. I did well in grad school and had some great job offers. I went back to visit and to learn even more from Ida Mae about eight times, and gathered enough stories from her to write yet another book. I could not stay away from her long. She became a very close friend of mine, and so did her family. We wrote to each other when we could, and I loved her letters that seemed to come from a time long ago.

I had a very lucrative job offer in Atlanta for a leading newspaper there, under normal circumstances I would have jumped at the offer, but I couldn't leave the mountains of West Virginia. I got a job teaching journalism at a West Virginia Community College, and taught a couple of summers at Virginia Tech and Radford. Naturally, I wrote for the *Charleston News Press* and a newspaper in Morgantown and Roanoke. I always felt that there was still another novel in me about the mountains around and eventually leading up to Slip Creek, especially since it stayed so alive in my mind. The stories were constantly with me.

I was in the middle of following a big story up in Pittsburg when a call came in from one of Ida Mae's grandchildren. He said that Ida Mae had passed away sitting on her porch one morning watching the sunrise. She made it to the ripe old age of 107. I took a vacation from my work and went to Slip Creek for the funeral. I flew into Bluefield, and rented a car and drove up the same road I did that wonderful day that I first met Ida Mae Cook, and the many times after that.

I remembered the way as if I had lived there. I drove straight to that little church up that dusty hollow. There wasn't a place to park near the church, I thought at first. There were family members directing and helping people park. They saw and recognized me, and had a special place for me to park behind the church. Cars were parked one-half mile down the road. There were reporters and TV cameras outside the church. There were about eleven long, black limousines, and the governor of the State of West Virginia and his family were there, and both senators, and the governor of Virginia, and the governor of Kentucky, and Sulie's family were there too. Ida Mae's sons saved me an honored seat up front, right behind the immediate family. There wasn't any room left inside the church, so they opened all the windows and doors, so the people left standing outside could hear the whole sermon and the music. Looking at the crowd, it seemed the whole county showed up for this grand "good-bye." Most of the people were her relatives and close friends. The choir sang, just as Ida Mae had wished, and her casket was plain and simple without frills, like Ida Mae.

The church members had a supper for all who attended, and there was plenty of food. I looked at Ida Mae, and she looked as if she finally got the rest she well deserved. She was dressed in the pretty blue dress with long sleeves and a high collar that she had chosen for her burial. She had her Bible in her hand and a picture of her family. She looked beautiful. I could not help but cry and was filled with hard emotion. I knew that I would miss my only link to living history, and my dear friend. How fortunate I was to know her and hear her stories through the years. You just can't read stories like that anymore. I had just talked to Ida Mae a couple of times on the phone this month, and she wanted me to come and spend another week with her. I am sorry now that I didn't. I did spend two full weeks with her last year though and gained eleven pounds.

A time to mourn, and a time to dance...

Everyone that stood around inside and outside the church had some story to tell about Ida Mae, and how she helped their family or helped them in other ways, and how she never turned anyone away from her door. She had helped doctor just about every child born in the holler, or had babysat most of them. All the mountain people were honestly saddened by her passing.

I got in line of the funeral procession, and the short winding trip was a sad but beautiful one. The autumn kissed trees seemed to bow as we passed with her coffin, and even the birds sat still. The hearse parked just outside of the rock wall surrounding the cemetery. The pallbearers, who were her grandsons and great-grandsons, gently lifted their light cargo and walked slowly up to the spot where Ida Mae would sleep with her beloved Sherman. The chairs from the funeral home were already there by the gravesite, and there was a canopy over them, and green felt carpet lay over the freshly up heaved earth. The family had me sit with them. When the family was seated, the preacher stood up, addressed her family, and told of the great loss we all felt, and the reward that Ida Mae was now receiving. The choir from the church sang without the accompaniment of the piano, and their voices sounded earthy yet heavenly and pure. I felt a close kinship with these people as my true mountain blood began to rise and be honored with them all. I was never so proud of my mountain roots as I was on that day.

Ida Mae was buried up on the mountain in the family cemetery not too far from her house, and now she is surrounded by all her loved ones. I was one of the lucky ones who heard first hand of the amazing cycle of life of Ida Mae Cook and her beloved family. When I looked into those liquid blue eyes and held her hand, she would smile when she talked about her life, and I saw those eyes cloud up like a summer rain when she talked about her loss of her soul mate, Sherman.

She may be gone in the flesh, but I know in my heart that she will continue watching out for her mountain kin and protecting her mountain love. She will always be in my heart as the most interesting and most loved teacher I ever had. As I got back into my car, I rolled down the windows, took a deep breath of the blessed air around me, and drove slowly down the mountain. I realized what a beautiful day it was, and the breeze was warm, carrying the smell of September. If I had the power, I would make sure that Ida Mae would be recognized as 'Saint Ida, Mother of the Mountain People.' I could not think of a better title to describe her.

Now, as I sit back and read the interview and listen to my little cassettes, read my later notes on her, I wish I had been there a hundred or so years ago to be with Ida Mae and her clan, and run through the hills, and be secluded like castaways on an island, beholding to no one and being self-sufficient. Life had to be hard, but they didn't know a simpler way or any other way. How pure and beautiful they must have been. No wonder God visited there often. Ida Mae showed me I had a big bucket, and it was up to only me to keep it filled, and I will use every ounce that bucket will hold.

Because of knowing her, I am a better man, and I will never look down my nose at anyone or feel greater than anyone else, and I will always remember that the Meades, Jewells and the Cook families were so special, and they were not dumb ignorant hicks, and they lived in the place where God walks to clear His mind. Why wasn't the rest of my school life this educational and this believable? I am so proud and humbled to have known this powerful lady, and to have been taught about a family's pride and legacy. I remembered our visits and how we would talk about my problems with college and with my professors, and she would guide me with her motherly way. She was a treasure chest of wisdom, and I thank God every day for being shown where the treasure lay.

Because of her journals, I started working on my family roots. I got other family members looking up their kin, and it has been great fun studying the names and dates, along with locations. One day when I find a wife and have children, I will teach them about their family, and hopefully, they will have the same feelings of pride about me as Ida Mae's had about her family, and as her children do about her. I will write in my journal every day, just as I have since the first day I sat on that long wooden porch, and heard about mysterious creatures, and dreamed about Indians as I sipped her wonderful iced tea.

Thank you, Ida Mae Cook!

The End

Ecclesiastes, of the King James Bible, chapter 3,
A Time for Everything, was used in between chapter breaks.
It seems that this section of the Bible is so appropriate
to an Appalachian Story. Don't you agree?

Teresa Stutso Jewell

About the Author

Teresa Stutso Jewell was born and raised in the middle of the Appalachian Coal Fields, in a small town of War, West Virginia. Her daddy was a hard-working, coal mining man, and her mom was a good, housewife and mother of four. She is of Italian and Scots-Irish decent. Teresa spent most of her childhood roaming the woods behind her house, and playing with her friends in what she thought was paradise. She was educated there in War, and was a hairdresser for about 37 years. Teresa married early, and has one son. It was in her beauty shop where her story telling and writing started. She would tell stories to her little customers to get them to hold still and be quiet while she was cutting their hair. The stories grew and so did Teresa's audience. So, she just turned her imagination inside out and began to write seriously. Teresa has a Facebook Page and can be reached by email at Teresastutsojewell@gmail.com.

***

Teresa Stutso Jewell will be publishing a book of poetry, *My Mountain Laurels*, a collection of short stories (not yet named), and a book about the Appalachian fairies, elves, sprites, and brownies.

CPSIA information can be obtained
at www.ICGtesting.com
Printed in the USA
LVHW032107040119
602824LV00007B/10/P